He held her against the lean length of his body

"A physical relationship between us would make a mockery of everything I believe that sort of closeness should mean between a man and a woman!"

His mouth lowered to claim hers. And as her lips parted moistly beneath his, Cassandra knew that she had only been fooling herself the last time he held her like this. She wanted this man—this man who was to be her husband!

She wrenched away from him at this realization, looking up into that hard, merciless face with wide, bewildered eyes. She didn't love Jonas, and yet she wanted him in a way that shocked and distressed her.

"May the mockery continue," Jonas finally responded.

CAROLE MORTIMER is the youngest of three children and grew up in a small Bedfordshire village with her parents and two brothers. She still loves nothing more than going "home" to visit her family. In her mid-thirties, she now has a husband, three very active sons, four cats and a dog, which doesn't leave her a lot of time for hobbies! Her strong, traditional stories, with their distinctly modern appeal, fascinating characters and involving plots, have earned her an enthusiastic audience worldwide.

Books by Carole Mortimer

HARLEQUIN PRESENTS PLUS

HARLEQUIN PRESENTS

Carole Mortimer

HUNTER'S MOON

Harlequin Books

TORONTO • NEW YORK • LONDON
AMSTERDAM • PARIS • SYDNEY • HAMBURG
STOCKHOLM • ATHENS • TOKYO • MILAN
MADRID • WARSAW • BUDAPEST • AUCKLAND

ISBN 0-373-11703-5

HUNTER'S MOON

CHAPTER ONE

'MUMMY...'

'Yes, darling?'

'Mummy, why is Uncle Jonas going to give Aunt Joy away? Don't we want her any more?'

'Out of the mouths of babes and innocents...' Cassandra had found her younger sister Joy a trial to be borne for longer than she cared to think about, but actually giving her away hadn't, she admitted ruefully, actually occurred to her!

But that wasn't quite, she realised as she slowly put her pencil down on the desk, abandoning the design she had been working on—for the moment—what her young daughter meant now either!

Bethany had been to her grandmother's for tea, and from this conversation Cassandra could see that the little girl had been indulging in one of her favourite pastimes—that of making herself as inconspicuous as possible while an adult conversation was taking place, and in so doing listening in on something that really was none of her business! It was the fault of the adults in question really, for forgetting Bethany was there, but nevertheless Cassandra usually gave her young daughter—a little over four years of age, and already precocious beyond belief, if equally adorable!—a sharp rebuke for the well-remembered, if less understood eavesdropping.

But this time, Cassandra had to admit, she was too interested in what Bethany had overheard to even think of the rebuke...

They were in the sitting-room that Cassandra also used as an office, part of the room given over to her drawing-board, the other kept as a cosy place for Bethany to join her and watch television or play with her toys if she wanted to. Tonight Bethany had the television on, sitting cross-legged on the carpet in front of it, but her attention wasn't on the hectic cartoon now showing, her elbows resting on her knees, her chin resting in her hands as she looked up at Cassandra, golden-brown eyes grave with puzzlement, long black hair kept tidily in plaits for school as they reached almost down to her tiny waist, still in this style, although Bethany had changed out of her school uniform when she returned from her grandmother's a little over an hour ago.

There was no doubting the relationship between mother and daughter, their colouring identical, Cassandra's midnight-black hair almost as long as her daughter's. But Bethany still maintained that childish chubbiness to her face that gave her such an endearing prettiness, whereas Cassandra was tall and reed-thin, with shadowed hollows to her cheeks and angled jaw, her beauty more hauntingly ethereal than glowingly lovely.

She smiled down at her daughter now, although inside she had stiffened defensively the moment Jonas's name was mentioned. 'Of course we want her, darling,' she dismissed lightly. 'What makes you think that we don't?'

Bethany screwed her face up expressively as she tried to remember exactly what she had overheard earlier this evening. 'Grandma said——' She broke off awkwardly, wincing guiltily at Cassandra for having given herself away in this way.

'It's all right, Bethany,' she smiled indulgently, too intrigued to issue any form of reprimand, even though she knew Bethany was expecting it. 'What did Grandma say...?'

'Well...' Bethany sat forward, her eyes glowing excitedly at this unexpected treat of actually being *invited* to relate gossip. 'While I was having tea with Grandma today she and Aunt Joy were talking and Grandma said...' She finally had to pause for breath. 'She said that dinner tonight was the perfect time for Aunt Joy to ask Uncle Jonas to give her away!' Bethany looked puzzled once again.

And Cassandra's heart sank as her worst fears were confirmed; she realised her sister Joy was going to ask Jonas to take their father's place at the Easter wedding she and her fiancé were planning. She was also filled with outrage, as her mother must know she would be—which was obviously why she hadn't been invited to dinner this evening too!—at the very idea of Jonas stepping into her father's shoes in any way.

'Has Grandma decided she doesn't want Aunt Joy any more?' Bethany persisted. 'Is that why Uncle Jonas is going to give her away?'

As far as Cassandra was concerned, she felt like giving the whole Kyle family away at this moment in time! This was obviously her mother's idea, to try and bring Jonas in as a member of the family rather than the business associate he would obviously prefer to be. And which Cassandra herself would prefer him to be too! She didn't doubt that her mother was also trying to heal the rift that had been between the two of them almost from the moment they met nine months ago after the death of Cassandra's husband—and Jonas's brother—Charles.

Cassandra could have told her mother to save herself the bother of even trying, if her mother had consulted her; the differences between Jonas and herself were irretrievable. But she understood exactly why her mother was trying to manoeuvre the situation; it would hardly be the done thing for the matron of honour and the man giving the bride away to launch into one of their verbal battles in the middle of the wedding planned for four months' time!

'Why are you smiling, Mummy?' Bethany had deserted the television completely now, having crossed the room to stand in front of Cassandra, one star-fish-shaped hand resting on one of her mother's denim-clad knees. 'It isn't funny... is it?'

Cassandra was smiling, with irony, an emotion Bethany was too young to appreciate just yet, because if she didn't smile she would cry! Her mother had arranged this so well, Christmas being exactly two weeks away, the last possible time of year for Cassandra to even think of creating difficulties between herself and the rest of her family, not for her own sake but for Bethany's. At almost any other time Cassandra wouldn't have hesitated about ringing her mother to tell her exactly what she thought of the idea of Jonas giving Joy away at the Easter wedding, and withdrawing as matron of honour if he was asked. But two weeks before Christmas, when she so wanted everything to go as smoothly as possible for Bethany during this, her first Christmas since

Charles had died, was not the time to create such awkwardness with the rest of the family.

It was very unfair of her mother, and Joy, who also knew exactly how she felt, to even be thinking of asking Jonas such a thing. Especially now. And while Cassandra appreciated that she couldn't make a scene over this now she could at least try to get her mother to delay asking Jonas until after the holiday period. Although, knowing her mother, she would realise exactly why Cassandra wanted her to delay, and go ahead and ask him anyway!

Her only consolation—if it could be called that!—was that she knew Jonas would hate being asked almost as much as she resented it! But he couldn't possibly hate it *as* much!

She deliberately turned her attention back to her beloved daughter now, for whom she would do anything— even grit her teeth and suffer through Jonas's visits here, which she did regularly, as he and Bethany had formed a bond as strong as the rift between him and Cassandra!—smiling down at her warmly. 'No, darling, it isn't funny,' she acknowledged ruefully, smoothing back the black fringe that framed the cherubic beauty of her daughter's face.

God, how Cassandra wished she had someone she could turn to now, someone to tell her what was the right thing to do in the tangled mess everything had become. This last ten months of being on her own with Bethany hadn't been the easiest of times for her, and some of the decisions she had made had turned out disastrously, both personally and professionally. Sometimes she just longed for someone to give her a hug, or her arm a squeeze, as they told her she was doing all right—

even if she knew the latter wasn't strictly true. And there
was no one—her mother and Joy were her only family
now, and after her mother's initial invitation for both
her and Bethany to move in with them, an invitation
Cassandra had had to refuse, and which, she knew, her
mother had taken as rejection, her sister and mother,
apart from the occasional invitation for Bethany to join
them for tea after school or an outing at the weekends,
had become wrapped up in their own lives once again,
rarely seeming to give a thought to Cassandra, Bethany's
mother, widowed at only twenty-four. Perhaps that was
her own fault; maybe she could have handled her refusal
of her mother's offer in a different way, but nevertheless——

God, she was starting to sound self-pitying now, she
realised with a defensive straightening of her spine, and
that would never do—even if her world did seem to be
crashing down about her ears. And she didn't doubt that
at the first sign of vulnerability on her part Jonas would
attack, as he had in the past, with all the razor-sharp
ferocity of which he was capable!

She could still recall—with complete clarity—the first
time she had met Jonas; it had also been the first occasion he had made her aware of just how con-
temptuous he was of her. There had been many occasions
since, but that one stood out in her mind for its sheer
cruelty!

Jonas hadn't returned to England for Charles's fu-
neral, having lived in America for the last twelve years,
and claiming on his return that he hadn't been informed
in time to attend the service, and so had seen no reason
to come to England after the event. Except that a month

after Charles's death the solicitors had called the family together to read the will, and Jonas's presence had been requested for that. It was noticeable that he made the effort to come back to England on *that* occasion!

Cassandra had still been numb from the shock of Charles's death and the consequences that had followed, had barely been aware of the fact when Charles's solicitor told her they had written to Jonas asking for him to be present. That numbness had fled with a vengeance when Jonas was shown into her lounge that day, Mr Harcourt believing this would be the best place for the reading of the will.

She had been alone in the room, none of the rest of the family having arrived yet, standing up slowly to greet the half-brother Charles had never had the chance to introduce her to. His appearance alone had come as something of a shock to her; she had expected him to look like Charles, she supposed, had even been guarding herself for the meeting, and instead she had found herself looking at a harshly dark man who bore no resemblance to Charles whatsoever.

Charles had been tall, blond-haired and blue-eyed, charming to both young and old in his desire to be liked. Apart from his equally impressive height, Jonas was the exact opposite of his half-brother: skin tanned darkly teak, saturnine almost, his hair as black as a moonless night, eyes equally black, lines of cynical hardness etched beside his nose and unsmiling mouth, giving him the appearance of being older than the thirty-five Cassandra knew him to be.

That hard black gaze had raked over her disparagingly as he took in the black sheath of a dress she wore, the starkness of the colour giving her pale skin a slightly sallow appearance. 'The grieving widow, I presume?' he drawled tauntingly once the door had closed behind the housekeeper as she left after showing him in.

Cassandra gasped at the insulting tone. She didn't even know this man, had no—— But perhaps she had misunderstood him; this was an awkward occasion, especially as the two of them had never met before.

She met his gaze steadily, looking gaunt with her hair secured back at her nape, even the light make-up she had applied that morning doing little to add colour to the hollowness of her cheeks. 'Yes, I'm Cassandra,' she confirmed huskily, holding out her hand in greeting. 'I'm sorry we had to meet in these circumstances,' she added politely, still waiting for him to take her hand.

'I doubt we would have met at all if it hadn't been "these circumstances",' he dismissed impatiently. 'Do you have any idea why I've been asked to attend this reading?' He looked at her with narrowed eyes, still ignoring her outstretched hand.

Cassandra let her arm fall back to her side, shaking her head slightly, looking at him frowningly. 'I'm afraid I don't,' she dismissed with a shrug. 'I presume it's because you've been named in the will——'

'Credit me with enough intelligence to know that, woman,' he cut in impatiently. 'I just wondered why the solicitors felt it necessary to bring me all the way over from the States for the damned thing, why they couldn't have just informed me by mail!'

'I believe it's usual to have everyone named in the will present at these things, if possible.' Cassandra was frowning with the effort of trying to deal with this man's aggression; it was the last thing she felt capable of coping with on top of everything else!

'I'm a busy man, Cassandra,' he snapped harshly.

'I'm sure that if you had explained——'

'Oh, I did,' he said in a tone that implied he had done much more than that! 'But I was told it was imperative that I be here.'

For the first time since Charles had died Cassandra felt an emotion other than that crippling numbness; she felt the beginnings of unease. 'They gave you no indication why...?'

'None at all.' His mouth twisted disgustedly. 'Although I believe we are about to find out...' he added softly as the door opened again to admit the solicitor, quickly followed by Cassandra's family.

And find out they did! Cassandra's numbness receded completely as the will was read, to be replaced by shock and disbelief. She couldn't believe what Charles had done!

Her mother seemed as stunned, and had to be almost physically helped from the house by Joy as the two women left almost immediately after the reading of the will. Which left Cassandra, once the solicitor had left, alone again with Jonas Hunter. And she knew even less what to say to him now than she had before!

Although she needn't have worried; he seemed more than capable of talking for the pair of them!

'Well, that must have come as something of a shock to you,' he drawled knowingly. 'Me too,' he murmured almost to himself, frowning, his attention suddenly returning to Cassandra with narrow-eyed assessment. 'I'm sure you must have thought you would automatically

inherit Charles's share of Hunter and Kyle after his
death?'

She had thought no such thing, as it happened, had
believed Bethany would be his sole heir, those shares put
in trust for her, under Cassandra's guidance, until she
was twenty-one. It was what she and Charles had always
discussed. Why had he chosen to change his mind, especially without telling her? She hadn't wanted any of
Charles's shares for herself; she already had the ten per
cent left to her by her father only two months before
Charles had died, a fact he had been very aware of.

But for Charles to have divided his thirty-five per cent
of the company shares, ten per cent put in trust for
Bethany, and the other twenty-five per cent to Jonas
Hunter——! She still couldn't take it in!

Charles hadn't even spoken to Jonas for years, had
made no further effort to contact his younger brother
after the other man had refused their wedding invitation—well, he hadn't exactly refused it; he had just
ignored it completely! Charles had certainly given her
no indication whatsoever that he intended, effectively,
making Jonas the holder of the single most shares in
Hunter and Kyle. Even though Cassandra had the voting
right over Bethany's ten per cent that still only gave her
twenty per cent to Jonas's twenty-five.

Her father and Charles had had an equal thirty-five
per cent of the shares of the company they had formed
together, putting the other thirty per cent on the open
market, confident that either of them had the majority
over the market, and together they had no fears of any
take-over bids.

But the death of Cassandra's father last New Year had divided his shares, giving Marguerite a fifteen per cent share, and Joy and Cassandra ten per cent each. Charles's death had now divided those family shares up even more, and in a way that had been totally unexpected, Cassandra readily admitted. Although Charles had to have known what he was doing. At least, she hoped he had!

She shrugged dismissively, determined this man shouldn't see just how shaken she was by Charles's will. 'They were Charles's shares; he was free to do what he wanted with them.'

'Because you already have what you wanted from your marriage to him?' Jonas said accusingly.

Her eyes widened. 'I married Charles because I loved him—— '

'Oh, come on, Cassandra.' Jonas's mouth twisted scornfully. 'Charles was twenty-five years older than you——'

'Twenty-three,' she defended, bright spots of colour now highlighting her cheeks. 'But that made no difference to how I felt about him——'

'I'll just bet it didn't.' He shook his head disgustedly. 'He was Charles Hunter, your father's business partner, could have been *forty* years older than you—and you would still have been willing to marry him!'

'You don't know what you're talking about!' she gasped at his insulting tone.

'Don't I?' he said softly, his eyes narrowed. 'But I know more about my famous sister-in-law than you perhaps realise,' he told her dismissively. 'Cassandra Kyle, the designer of exclusive clothes for the woman

with plenty of money! And you owe it all to Charles,'
he scorned.

Charles *had* been responsible for helping her open her
first boutique in London, she admitted that, knew that
without his help she would probably have remained an
unknown for a lot more years than she had. And considering the way her business was now, the state of the
economy meaning that those women with plenty of
money were a lot less well off than they used to be,
perhaps it might have been better if she had *remained*
unknown! But that seemed to be something Jonas
Hunter didn't know! She wondered for how long...

'Poor Charles,' Jonas drawled. 'I could almost feel
sorry for the poor besotted fool he must have become!
Admittedly you're beautiful enough, but I credited my
self-centred brother with more sense than to go for that
older-man-falling-for-younger-woman trick.' He shook
his head scathingly. 'Hunter became the hunted,' he
added softly, the slow deliberation with which he delivered the words giving them the full insult he intended
them to have.

Cassandra paled. 'Get out,' she told him shakily. 'Get
out of my home!' She was trembling so badly that she
felt as if she might collapse. And she refused to do that
in front of this hateful man!

'Oh, I'm going, Cassandra,' he assured her drily. 'In
fact, I'm going back to the States for a while to sort
things out over there. But I'll be back,' he told her softly.
'I'll be back...' It was a threat as well as a promise!

And two months later he had been, taking over as
head of Hunter and Kyle. And Cassandra hated seeing
him there, hated him for the way he never lost an op-

portunity during the following months to torment her anew with those accusations...

Bethany still looked slightly confused even once Cassandra had explained the formality of Joy's future wedding to her, the necessity for Joy to be 'given away' by a member of her family if possible, a close friend if not; Cassandra wasn't sure which category Jonas came under! And Bethany was easily distracted from the subject altogether once Cassandra had mentioned something she *did* understand: bathtime!

As far as Bethany was concerned, the huge oval jacuzzi in her parents' bathroom had been put there solely for her to romp around in, the bubbles created from the surging foam and the scented liquid Cassandra had been persuaded to put in soon up to her small pointed chin as she played games with their rainbow brightness.

As her young daughter played with squealing delight, Cassandra stood in the adjoining bedroom looking through her wardrobe for something to wear when she visited her mother that evening, because even though she wasn't going to join them for dinner—she already had a dinner engagement—she wasn't prepared to let Marguerite get away with this as easily as all that, and intended calling at her mother's house on her way out. And if Jonas should arrive while she was talking to her mother he would no doubt look at her with his usual criticism—hence her frowning attention on what to wear. If she chose something that would flatter her slender darkness then Jonas would treat her scornfully, and if she chose something demure he would deride the effort as being a false one. She had never been able to win with

Jonas. He had formed an opinion of her before they even met, because she had been the wife of the brother he despised, and to give him his due it had never wavered; he despised her as much as he had Charles. Cassandra had formed a similar opinion of him after their first meeting, which had also never wavered—how could it when he had treated her with such contempt on that occasion, and every one since?

Jonas's only redeeming quality, as far as she was concerned, was that his dislike of her didn't extend as far as her daughter; he openly adored Bethany. And Bethany reciprocated by believing him to be the most wonderful man in the world. Cassandra could only hope that her daughter's taste in men improved before she reached maturity!

'Wear the yellow dress.' Bethany grinned at her enchantingly from the bath. 'The one Daddy liked,' she added softly, sadness entering the golden-brown of her eyes at this mention of her father.

Cassandra's own hand shook slightly as she reached out automatically for the dull gold gown that Charles had so liked to see her in, its clinging style to just above her knees, her shoulders left completely bare, classically and timelessly appealing. Charles had always claimed it gave her eyes a golden glimmer that matched the colour of the dress, and for a brief moment after Bethany had called out to her it had almost seemed as if Charles himself spoke to her.

'Yes—wear the pale gold,' a voice echoed mockingly. 'You look like a high priestess in it!'

Cassandra spun round with a gasp. This second voice was certainly nothing like Charles speaking to her; irresponsibly charming Charles had certainly never spoken to her in that disparaging way! Nor did the man who stood so arrogantly in the open bedroom doorway look anything like the husband Cassandra had loved in spite of his reckless disregard for what he termed 'tomorrow'. It could take care of itself, he had always claimed with that boyish grin of his. Only he wasn't here to see 'tomorrow' with her; this man was!

Jonas Hunter. Charles's younger half-brother, the two of them the products of their father's two marriages. And Charles and Jonas were as different as night and day, as shadow and sunlight. And there was no confusion in Cassandra's mind, at least, which man was which!

CHAPTER TWO

CASSANDRA looked warily across the room at Jonas, and knew that, despite his height and size, he could move with an animal stealth that was completely unnerving. Which was why she hadn't heard his approach to her bedroom just now, she realised with deep resentment. This man aroused many emotions in her, and although most people seemed in awe of him no one she knew who had met him seemed to quite know how they felt about him—liking seeming too insipid an emotion to use in connection with this man. People would either love or loathe him, Cassandra would hazard a guess, having no doubt which emotion she herself felt towards him! Or perhaps it was *because* most other people were so much in awe of his arrogant power that they chose not to voice an opinion about how they felt about him!

'Mrs Humphries let me in,' he drawled now before Cassandra could voice her displeasure at this blatant intrusion into her home. 'She told me Bethany was having her bath, and when she was called away to answer the telephone I took it upon myself to come upstairs.' Dark brows were raised in silent challenge as he dared her to question his arrogance.

This man 'took it upon himself' to do exactly what he wanted whenever he wanted, Cassandra knew—but he wasn't about to start walking about her house, the home she had shared with Charles for the five years of their marriage, as if he owned it! Which he most certainly did not. Jonas might have inherited a lot of things from Charles when he died, but this house was not one of them.

Her eyes flashed deeply gold. 'You——'

'Uncle Jonas! Uncle Jonas!' An ecstatic Bethany came bounding out of the bathroom to launch herself at Jonas, effectively cutting off any angry rebuke Cassandra might have been—damn it, *had* been—about to administer. 'It *is* you.' Bethany grinned at him gleefully.

Jonas had swung the little girl up in his arms by this time, uncaring of the water and bubbles that instantly soaked into his expensively tailored suit, obviously having come here straight from the office, by the formality of his clothing. 'Hussy!' Jonas laughed huskily as he buried his face in the damp darkness of Bethany's hair.

Cassandra watched the closeness between the two of them with mixed emotions—amazement at the way Jonas lost all trace of that hard cynicism and reserve when it came to Bethany, resentment at that very closeness which had seemed instantaneous from the very moment the two set eyes on each other, while at the same time grateful that Bethany did have this male influence in her young life. Because Bethany's other contacts in life were mainly women: Cassandra, her aunt and grandmother, the housekeeper, Jean Humphries; even Bethany's formteacher at the day-school she had begun attending in September was a kindly middle-aged lady. But none the less Cassandra could still only deplore her daughter's choice of a man to adore!

But adore Jonas she did, and Cassandra moved into the adjoining bathroom to escape the painful sight of

Bethany in her uncle's arms, gathering up one of the thick peach-coloured towels to take it back into the bedroom. 'Here.' She held the towel out somewhat impatiently, avoiding Jonas's darkly taunting gaze as he mockingly noted the way Cassandra carefully avoided any contact with him while she wrapped Bethany in the sumptuous bath-towel. 'Your suit will be ruined,' she muttered defensively—she always seemed to be on the defensive where this man was concerned, had been made to feel that way from the very first time they met, and Jonas had never done anything to make her less wary and angry with him than she had been on that occasion.

'I can always buy a new suit,' Jonas drawled derisively. 'A cuddle with this particular young lady——' he tickled Bethany pointedly '—is priceless!'

Amazing how, even when she tried to make an effort with this man, he somehow managed to twist it round so that she appeared the one in the wrong again! Although if she was honest—with herself, at least—she hadn't really been thinking of him and his damned expensively hand-made suit at all when she got the towel, had actually resented his presence here, but most of all she had hated his easy laughter with Bethany. It was wrong of her, she knew, but when she looked at him with Bethany she felt he had no right to be there at all. But Bethany did love him so, to the point where Cassandra feared he was superseding Charles in her daughter's affections. Deliberately so on Jonas's part...?

Jonas had always been the black sheep of Charles's family from the little she had gathered from either Charles or his father, Jonas's mother having been divorced by Peter Hunter years before Jonas reached adulthood. Jonas, it appeared, had lived in America for years without making any effort to see either Charles or their father. Cassandra had realised exactly what sort of man he was when he didn't even come to their wedding, even though Charles had expressed a wish that he be his best man. Maybe his refusal to be with his own brother on his wedding day was another one of the reasons she now felt so resentful about the part he was going to be asked to play in her sister Joy's wedding...

'Don't you think so?'

She looked up sharply, to find Jonas looking down at her probingly; despite her own considerable height, he was still at least six inches taller than her.

'Bethany's hugs are priceless,' he reminded her of what he had said only minutes ago, holding Bethany easily in one arm as he did so.

'Absolutely,' Cassandra agreed in a briskly dismissive voice, lifting her daughter down on to the carpeted floor. 'Time we got you into some clothes, young lady, before you get cold,' she explained with a smile as Bethany looked disappointed. 'I—— Ah, Jean,' she said with some relief as she spied her housekeeper standing in the doorway Jonas had so recently vacated.

The older woman, in her early sixties now, Cassandra suddenly realised with a frown, looked slightly harassed as she glanced at Jonas before speaking. 'I was just on my way upstairs to tell you Mr Hunter was here, when the telephone began to ring.' She gave Cassandra an apologetic grimace, obviously feeling responsible for Jonas's arrogant intrusion upstairs; if they had been alone, Cassandra would have assured the woman who had become her friend during the last five years that she was well aware Jean would have been trying to stop the equivalent of a tank in trying to prevent Jonas from doing exactly as he pleased! Although she knew that, given the opportunity, Jean would have had a good try, none the less!

The two women had had severe differences when Cassandra had first become Charles's wife. Jean had been in charge of Charles's household for years when he and Cassandra married; until that time, it seemed, Charles had given every impression of remaining a carefree bachelor, and at already forty-two that perhaps wasn't such a strange assumption to have made. But it had meant, when he had married Cassandra, that the older woman deeply resented the introduction of a twenty-year-old bride as new mistress of the house. Naturally so, of course.

Cassandra hadn't blamed the other woman for feeling that way at all, had tried very hard, during those first few months, not to step on the other woman's already bruised feelings, determined that Charles shouldn't be made to feel he was living in the middle of a battle-field—worse than that, that he might actually have to take sides! That was the last thing Cassandra wanted for him, because she knew that he would hate that, that he hated any sort of upset in his usually smooth-running existence. In fact, Cassandra had teased him that it had been for that very reason he had balked against marrying her at all for months after they had realised they were in love. He had protested that it wasn't that at all, that he felt perhaps the age-difference was too much, that it would eventually break them up. Cassandra's answer to that had been but think of what a marvellous time they would have had together, for however long it lasted. Charles's love for her hadn't been strong enough to fight such an argument, thank God, and Cassandra knew, despite that slightly reckless air of his that could make him so frustratingly irresponsible, that they had shared five good years together.

But those first few months of being Charles's wife, because it seemed Jean Humphries would never accept her, had been traumatic ones for Cassandra. And then Cassandra had done something that had forever changed her relationship with Jean—she had produced Bethany... Jean doted on the little girl from the day Cassandra came home from the hospital with her, Bethany being the closest thing the older woman would ever have to a grandchild of her own. For the title of Mrs was only a professional one for Jean, Cassandra knew, the other woman never having been married.

During the months since Charles's death, and the problems that had followed, Jean had come to be so much more than just a friend to Cassandra too; she had been the comforting mother she had needed so badly and which her own mother hadn't been able to be.

Cassandra gave Jean a wan smile now, knowing just how impossible it would have been to stop Jonas from coming up here. 'Jonas decided he would like to come up and see Bethany take her bath,' she accepted dismissively. 'If you would like to warm Bethany's milk for her, and perhaps a pot of coffee for us...?' She looked enquiringly at Jonas as she made the last request; the last thing she actually wanted was to share a cosy pot of coffee with him, but she couldn't escape the fact that Bethany would probably be so disappointed that it would be hell on earth trying to get her to bed after Jonas had left!

Her hope that Jonas might refuse the invitation was dashed when he gave a mocking inclination of his head.

'Sorry to disappoint you,' he murmured derisively once Jean had gone to get the drinks and Bethany had returned to the bathroom to dry herself and dress in her pyjamas and dressing-gown ready for bed, his mouth twisting wryly. 'But I came here straight from the office, and after the day I've had I could do with the caffeine,' he added grimly, running a hand over the tension of his brow.

Cassandra gave him a searching look. He did look strained, his black-rimmed glasses, glasses he rarely wore, she recalled, partly concealing those hard black eyes. 'Things not running smoothly at the office?' she returned lightly, although inwardly she had tensed once again; what had happened to cause those extra lines of strain beside his nose and mouth tonight?

His expression sharpened with harsh derision. 'Do you really care?'

Her eyes flashed deeply gold at his scorn. 'Of course I—— Must I remind you that Hunter and Kyle is as much my concern as it is yours?' she challenged in a reasoning tone.

Jonas returned her gaze speculatively. 'Is it?'

'You know it——' She abruptly broke off her sharp retort as Bethany came trotting in unconcernedly from the bathroom, dressed in her nightclothes now, and stood expectantly in front of Cassandra as she waited for the nightly ritual of having her hair brushed.

'Uncle Jonas...' she began tentatively as Cassandra made the steady strokes through her hair with the brush. 'Uncle Jonas, do you believe in Father Christmas?' She frowned across the room at him as he sat in the bedroom chair now watching them.

Cassandra stopped the brushing to look down at her daughter in some surprise; this was the first indication she had ever had that Bethany was even beginning to doubt the myth! Of course, once a child started school, it was difficult to stop older children from telling her the truth, but even so they had gone through all the usual rituals together this year—the letter to Santa with a list of what Bethany would like for Christmas this year dutifully sent off to the North Pole, the trip to see a Father Christmas, in a well-known shop, that Bethany had known wasn't the real one, but who she believed could pass a message on to him, just in case her letter should go astray. Bethany had helped Jean in the kitchen while she made mince pies, one of which was to be placed on a plate on Christmas Eve, along with eight carrots—one for each of the reindeer—and she had also checked the sherry supply, so that they could leave a glassful out with the mince pie, to warm the poor man on his busy round. In actual fact, either Cassandra or Jean would end up drinking the latter, depending on which of them felt more in need of it after the last-minute rush of getting everything arranged under the tree for the next morning when Bethany woke them at some ungodly hour so that they could go downstairs and see if Father Christmas had been yet!

All of which made Bethany's apparent doubt now more than a little puzzling...

Jonas looked taken aback by the question too. 'Why do you ask, poppet?' he avoided warily.

Bethany still looked thoughtful. 'Well, Father Christmas only brings you presents if you believe in him—and I would so like you to get lots and lots of presents, Uncle Jonas!' She grinned at him endearingly, at the same time dispelling any doubts Cassandra might have had about her own belief in Father Christmas! 'Mummy always does,' she confided excitedly.

Because Charles, despite her protests, had always swamped her with gifts, and not just at Christmas. Even though she had protested at the expense, assuring him she didn't need any of the things, he had begun showering her with jewellery, clothes, cars, anything he thought would give her pleasure, to the extent where Cassandra had begun to think he got more pleasure from giving her the things than she did receiving them...

But there would be no gifts from Charles for her to protest at this year. In fact, for Cassandra, the whole festive season was filled with unhappiness. A year ago on New Year's Eve, drunken revellers had crashed into her father's car and killed him instantly, and within weeks, it seemed—eight exactly, Cassandra knew—Charles had been dead too, from a massive heart attack that had given them no warning of its imminence.

No, there would be no outrageously extravagant gifts under the tree for her from Charles this year. Not that she would miss them; she would gladly have given away everything Charles had ever given her if she could have sorted out the financial mess her life had become during the last year. But none of those things would have been enough to solve that!

Jonas saw the shadows in her eyes, guessing, she was sure, only half the reason for her unhappiness. Jonas believed she had only married his brother for his money anyway, so there was no point in even trying to explain the truth of things to him!

'I bet if you stayed here with us Christmas night Father Christmas would leave you lots of presents too!' Bethany burst out expectantly. 'Ouch, that hurt, Mummy!' she protested indignantly as Cassandra dug the brush into her scalp.

'Sorry, darling,' Cassandra told her distractedly as she carefully untangled the brush from the glossy black locks, all the time fighting back her inward panic that Bethany should have said such a thing. She was sure Jonas had no more wish to stay here with them at Christmas than she did to have him here—she also knew he was bloody-minded enough to accept the suggestion just because he knew how much it would upset her if he did!

'Do you really think so, Bethany?' he thoughtfully answered the child, but his gaze was fixed on Cassandra's flushed face, tauntingly so.

'Oh, yes,' Bethany nodded with certainty, her expression so gravely intent that it was endearingly appealing—even to Cassandra, who felt like strangling her at this moment! 'So will you, Uncle Jonas? Stay here, I mean. We have lots of rooms, and—and I would like you to!' she added earnestly.

Cassandra looked at Jonas in dismay, wondering how he was going to withstand such an appeal; she knew she was already resigned now to having Jonas here if that was what Bethany really wanted and Jonas was agreeable. Even though she personally would hate every minute of it she would willingly do it if it would make Bethany happy——

A fact Jonas was very much aware of as he watched the emotions flickering across her face with knowing mockery—although his expression softened, became almost gentle, as he went down on one knee beside the standing Bethany, putting their faces on the same level, one of his arms going about her tiny waist as he cradled her to his side. 'That really is very kind of you to think of me in that way, Bethany,' he told her gruffly. 'Of both of you,' he couldn't resist adding with a challenging glint in his eyes for Cassandra. 'But I'm afraid,' he drawled with slow torture—for Cassandra, 'that I've already left my note out for Father Christmas, and so he will be expecting me to be at my apartment on Christmas night.'

'Oh, but that's easy,' Bethany told him in a pipingly confident voice. 'You just put out another note for him telling him where you will be. We did it last year when we went to Grandma's house.'

It was Cassandra's turn to raise black brows derisively this time, in answer to Jonas's accusing look for her previous year's efficiency. Well, what had she been supposed to do in that situation? Children worried, needed an explanation for such things, and that second note to Father Christmas last year had seemed the only answer when they were invited to spend Christmas with her parents. In the light of what had happened in the New Year, she was so grateful that she, Charles and Bethany had spent that last Christmas with both her parents...

'How clever of you.' Jonas's teasing attention returned to Bethany. 'And it really is a very good idea.

But actually I have to go and see your grandfather Peter on Christmas Eve.' He shook his head disappointedly. 'He's on his own too, you see, and he shouldn't really be on his own at Christmas, should he?' Jonas reasoned gently.

And Cassandra couldn't help wondering just how much time Jonas actually intended spending with his father on Christmas Eve; not very much, if any, she was sure. The two had met rarely since Jonas's return, and she didn't think the season of Christmas would make too much difference to their strained relationship. She was taking Bethany down to see her grandfather on Boxing Day, once some of the excitement for Bethany had died down; Peter was frail and old now, and young company tended to tire him more than any other.

'No,' Bethany accepted, although she had to blink back tears of disappointment at Jonas's not being with them after all. 'But I wish you could live here with us, Uncle Jonas.' Her bottom lip still trembling emotionally.

Cassandra almost choked! 'Bethany——'

Jonas shook his head, smiling ruefully. 'I'll see you later on Christmas Day, at your grandmother's house, and you can tell me all about your Christmas presents,' he cajoled brightly. 'I've been invited for lunch.'

Yet more news for Cassandra! What on earth did her mother think she was doing? Jonas wasn't family, was no relation to her mother whatsoever, and his connection to Cassandra was tenuous to say the least—a half-brother-in-law who had refused to even come to her wedding and had been nothing but objectionable since he had exploded into their lives a little over nine months ago! The unavoidable connection they all had with him through business certainly didn't mean that any of them had to be this friendly with him on a social level. Christmas Day at her mother's without her father's calming presence was going to be bad enough, but to now find Jonas was going to be there too...!

Only Bethany looked thrilled by the news, throwing her arms about Jonas's neck to hug him. 'All of us together for Christmas!' she glowed, clapping her hands with excitement now. 'That's the next best thing to having you live with us. I'm going to tell Mrs Humphries what a lovely Christmas we're all going to have!' She ran out of the room, hair flying, tendrils still slightly damp at the bottom where they had had a wetting in the bath.

A heavy, oppressive silence followed Bethany's departure, and with a weary sigh Cassandra turned to look at Jonas—— And then wished she hadn't! He stood in the doorway again now, leaning back against the door-frame, arms folded across his chest, mouth twisted tauntingly, eyes darkly mocking behind those somewhat protective glasses—not that this man needed protecting, from anything! Arrogant. Despicable. Ruthless. The adjectives she could find to describe this man were endless.

'I can see you're absolutely thrilled at the prospect of all of us being together on Christmas Day too!' he scorned in that harshly derisive voice of his that so grated on her.

'Thrilled' in no way described how she felt about spending Christmas Day in this man's company; she was absolutely horrified at the thought of spending that day of 'peace on earth and goodwill to all men' with this particular man!

'Bethany will like it,' she said dismissively—it was the only positive thing she could find to say about it!—as she placed the brush carefully back on the dressing-table with the rest of the gold-trimmed set, needlessly straightening the already neatly placed comb and hand-mirror. But she desperately needed something to occupy her hands— she was more than a little unnerved now at Jonas's presence here alone with her, in the bedroom she had shared with Charles for all of their marriage. 'Just as I ~w she appreciates your coming here to see her, as ⁄e tonight,' Cassandra continued determinedly, ⁄, with this man here, to even glance at the huge -poster bed—a wedding present from Charles to ⁄—that was usually so dominating in the room; this ⁄vening this man dominated it!

'But I didn't come here to see Bethany tonight,' Jonas told her softly. 'Much as I enjoy her company too,' he shrugged dismissively.

Cassandra gave him a sharp, frowning look. 'No?' she said warily.

'No,' he echoed tauntingly, straightening suddenly, even the mocking humour erased from his face now. 'As you're the other major shareholder in Hunter and Kyle, I thought you should know that I have just had an internal audit done of the company.'

Cassandra stared at him. 'You didn't mention this before...'

'No,' he acknowledged grimly. 'I didn't believe there was any need to; I ordered it as a matter of course now that I've been in charge of things for six months. I just wanted to be ready for the end of the tax year, although there didn't appear to be any problems. I say "appear to be''——' he met her gaze with steady intent '—because now I know differently.'

Cassandra swallowed hard, even as she felt all the colour drain from her face.

CHAPTER THREE

'DID you hear me, Cassandra?' Jonas rasped coldly. 'I said——'

'I heard you!' She turned away, totally shaken by this. She had known it had to come, of course, had realised it had to, but with the mess her own company had become she hadn't had the chance—or time!—to think about Hunter and Kyle. And she should have done, the dangerous intent in this man's eyes warned her harshly, when she risked another glance at him. She gripped her hands tightly together in front of her to stop their trembling. 'It was——'

'Mummy, Uncle Jonas, don't you want your coffee?' Bethany protested as she came bounding into the room to frown up at them impatiently for their delay.

'I would love some.' Jonas was the one to answer her, glancing at the plain gold watch with its leather strap. 'Unfortunately, I don't have the time now,' he refused with a disappointed grimace, his eyes narrowed as he glanced across at the still pale Cassandra. 'Marguerite has invited me to dinner tonight too,' he told her softly.

He thought she was going to be at her mother's for dinner, Cassandra realised. Thank God she wasn't; there was no way she could have given even a semblance of normality tonight at one of her mother's dinner parties, not after what this man had just told her.

And Cassandra knew exactly why Jonas had been invited to dinner tonight. It wasn't just that her mother wanted to ask Jonas to give Joy away at the wedding—although God knew that was bad enough. No, her mother was very much aware that Jonas was now head of Hunter and Kyle, and as such he was responsible for any profits the company might make, profits she and Joy had a share in. She wouldn't put it past her mother and Joy to have plans for Joy's fiancé Colin either—he *was* Jonas's assistant, and neither Marguerite nor Joy would be happy with him remaining just that, Cassandra was sure.

The knowing look in Jonas's eyes, when she looked up to make a reply, said he knew perfectly well of her mother and Joy's ambitions for Colin—also that he would do what he damned well pleased about that situation!

'That's nice,' Cassandra finally replied distractedly.

Jonas gave a taunting smile. 'Is it?'

She was tempted to tell him she didn't give a damn whether he went to her mother's for dinner every night of the week—as long as she didn't have to be there too! But Bethany clasped his hand at that moment, diverting his attention to her, and also putting an end to the conversation.

Bethany hung on to Jonas until the very last minute, making it impossible for Cassandra and Jonas to talk privately again. Cassandra was glad of the respite, and she knew Jonas wasn't bothered by the delay, because he expected to be talking to her again later on this evening. Cassandra shivered, glad once again that she had made other plans.

Bethany turned away now from the door where she had been standing forlornly waving to her uncle until the tail-lights of his car had completely disappeared. '*Can't* Uncle Jonas come and live with us?' She looked up at Cassandra appealingly.

Cassandra had been deep in thought, but this brought her sharply back into the present. This was the second time tonight her young daughter had made such a statement, and the sooner she was firmly told it wasn't even a possibility, the better! 'I wanted to talk to you about that, darling,' she told Bethany firmly as she sat her down in one of the armchairs.

It was still quite early when Cassandra arrived at her mother's house—deliberately so on her part; she was determined she wouldn't run into Jonas there now.

Her mother, she was informed, was still dressing for dinner, and so Cassandra sat down to wait for her. It was more imperative than ever that Jonas not be drawn any deeper into their personal lives than he already was; the man had the power—and the ruthlessness!—to destroy all of them, if he chose to do so.

Her mother was a good hostess; she had a fire burning brightly in the hearth to give the elegant lounge, with its pale cream and peach décor, a welcoming warmth, the family dining table, rather than the large formal one in a separate room, laid for dinner, the silver shining brightly, the crystal wine glasses sparkling in the firelight, the delicate posy of roses in the centre of the table perfectly matching the peach and cream in the rest of the room.

Cassandra stood up as her mother came into the room; she was much taller than her petite mother, and their colouring was completely different too, her mother's auburn hair going graciously—and expertly!—grey now. Joy looked the most like their mother; both women were short and slim, with beautifully even features, eyes a deep blue. But her mother and Joy, her two closest relatives, had always seemed a little like an alien species to Cassandra.

They lived their lives on such a superficial level, going to the beauty salon twice a week, lunching with friends, being seen in all the 'right' places, knowing all the 'right' people, likewise wearing all the 'right' clothes, both of them always immaculately dressed for the occasion. And both of them would recoil in horror at the mere suggestion that they should ever actually work a single day of their lives to pay for all that luxury they took so much for granted! Cassandra had always stood out like a duckling among such beautifully elegant swans...

She had never been able to understand how her mother and Joy could live such vacuous lives. But if she felt that way about them she knew her mother didn't understand her way of life any better. Her mother had given up on Cassandra when, at the age of seventeen, she had insisted on going to art college rather than the exclusive finishing-school her parents had picked out in Switzerland for their two daughters. Even worse, when Cassandra had left college two years later, she had gone to work for a major London fashion house, not as a model or designer herself, but as assistant to a designer. Humble beginnings—much to her mother's obvious disgust; there had never been anything humble about either Marguerite or Joy Kyle!

Even the relative success she had had as a designer herself hadn't exactly redeemed her in her mother's eyes: she still *worked* for a living. But at least Cassandra's choice of husband, after years of having her actions looked on with dismay, had met with her mother's approval—although even that new-found respectability had taken a knock in her mother's eyes, she knew, when Charles had died so suddenly: it simply wasn't the done thing to become a widow at only twenty-four years of age!

Her mother looked as graciously lovely as usual this evening, her auburn hair elegantly grey at the temples, her black below-the-knee dress perfect for this small family dinner-party—although she looked slightly disconcerted to see that Cassandra was also dressed for dinner, wearing the pale gold gown Bethany had requested.

Cassandra smiled, taking pity on her mother. 'Don't worry, I'm not gatecrashing your dinner party; I'm going on somewhere.'

Her mother couldn't quite hide her relief. 'You're welcome to join us if you would like to,' she said politely now that she knew Cassandra had no intention of staying.

Cassandra's smile widened. 'No, thanks. I'm meeting Simeon later——'

'Oh, really, Cassandra.' Her mother looked irritated now. 'That dreadful young man!'

That 'dreadful young man', her own assistant at the salon she ran in town still, had helped get her through the last difficult months. But he wasn't 'top-drawer' enough for her mother, coming from a working-class background; it didn't matter that he was also kind and caring, and that Cassandra liked him very much.

'Never mind Simeon,' she dismissed lightly. 'He isn't the reason I'm here.' She glanced across at the intimately laid dinner table. 'Five places, Mother?'

Her mother looked disconcerted again. 'Godfrey is joining us for dinner,' she dismissed.

'Us' was obviously Joy, Colin, and Marguerite. Godfrey Chorley was an old family friend who had become very helpful to her mother as a partner for social evenings since the death of her husband a year ago. At almost sixty, Godfrey seemed a confirmed bachelor, and after only a few minutes spent it his company it was easy to see why: Godfrey, as fond as Cassandra was of him, was easily the most boring man she had ever met!

Cassandra arched black brows. 'And the fifth?'

'Jonas,' her mother supplied offhandedly. 'I do feel so sorry for the dear man; he seems to know so few people in England, and——'

'Spare me that, please, Mother,' Cassandra cut in impatiently. 'If Jonas spends a lot of his time alone, it's because he chooses to,' she said knowingly; Jonas, for all his coldness with her, was an extremely attractive man, could have his pick of women to share his life.

'Well, anyway, he's coming to dinner this evening too,' her mother announced almost challengingly—a challenge Cassandra was only too happy to meet!

'Why?' she prompted softly.

'I've just——'

'Why, Mother?' she repeated firmly, easily meeting her mother's searching gaze.

'Bethany!' her mother finally realised. 'She was here earlier when we were discussing...! Joy has a perfect right to ask whom she wants to give her away,' she said in defence of her youngest daughter.

'It wasn't so long ago Joy was chasing after Jonas for quite another reason,' Cassandra reminded her drily, perfectly aware that when Jonas had first returned to England her sister had been very attracted to him indeed. But while Jonas hadn't seemed averse to having Joy reacquaint him with London he hadn't been interested in anything more than that from her, Joy had told her disappointedly one day. Cassandra had been most embarrassed by the whole incident; she had been sure Jonas was secretly laughing at them all for her sister's obvious ambitions where he was concerned. Joy's engagement to Colin was a relatively new thing, and Cassandra just hoped it was for the right reasons; Colin was nowhere near as 'primitively exciting' as Joy had claimed she thought Jonas was! Still, that was Joy's problem, not hers. Her problems were much more pressing than that.

'And if she had succeeded it might just have been the answer for all of us,' her mother snapped angrily.

Cassandra looked at her mother closely. 'And just what do you mean by that remark?'

'Isn't it obvious?' her mother said with impatient dismissal—although she wasn't quite meeting Cassandra's gaze, she noticed with a frown. Did her mother know more than she was prepared to say...?

'It would have been the perfect arrangement if we could have kept the company in the family,' her mother continued briskly. 'As it is, Jonas could eventually marry anybody, and then where will we all be?' She frowned.

Exactly where they were now, Cassandra would have thought. Unless her mother did know something...

'Don't start being difficult about this, Cassandra,' her mother told her shortly. 'The decision has been made, and nothing you say will make any difference.'

'But do you have to ask him now?' She frowned. 'What's the urgency?'

'There is no urgency,' her mother shrugged. 'We just thought it would be a nice gesture, what with the time of year and everything.'

A time of year when Jonas was much less likely to refuse, Cassandra realised ruefully, her own hands tied for very much the same reason. 'Mother——'

'Do stop calling me Mother in that disapproving way of yours,' she was told impatiently. 'Either Mummy, or Marguerite, if you prefer, but Mother makes me sound like some matriarchal monster!'

Her mother was tense and agitated, she could see. Admittedly, she also having been widowed, the last year had been as difficult for her mother as it had for her, but at the same time her mother had seemed to be coping, her life continuing to run in its usually smooth way. What had happened to change that? Unless her mother *did* know something. Colin was Jonas's assistant, so he would know all about the audit Jonas had ordered. Maybe that was why——

'Mr Chorley, madam,' the butler came into the room to announce after knocking quietly.

'Thank you, Jenkins,' she accepted vaguely. 'Show him in, will you?' She turned to Cassandra once they were alone again. 'Just drop this for now, Cassandra,' she hissed impatiently. 'It's absolutely none of Godfrey's business.'

'I would have thought Godfrey was the more obvious choice to give Joy away,' she began reasoningly. 'He——'

'He's a family friend, nothing more,' her mother snapped. 'Even if he would like to be more than that. *Especially* as he would like to be more than that.' She was becoming agitated once again. 'Cassandra, Jonas is very important to all our lives, so please just stop being difficult where he's concerned!' she pleaded anxiously.

Cassandra was prevented from saying anything more on the subject by Godfrey's arrival, quickly followed by Joy and Colin joining them. As it could only be a matter of minutes before Jonas arrived too she quickly made her excuses!

But she was so preoccupied when she finally met Simeon at the restaurant that she couldn't have been much company for him. Not that he complained; they didn't have that sort of relationship—Simeon was more like a brother to her than anything else, despite what the rest of the family might think to the contrary.

Simeon had turned up at her London salon one day three years ago, short and dark-haired, at twenty-six nevertheless managing to look perpetually boyish, with no qualifications except a wonderful eye for colour and design, a fact he had proved only too well when on that very first occasion he had told her her displays were all wrong and offered to do them for her! The difference he had made in a very short time had convinced her she should employ him. It was a decision she had never regretted—although not even Simeon's obvious talents could alter the fact that her business was in deep financial trouble. She wasn't even sure she would be able to continue to employ him after the expense of putting out the spring collection!

But because Cassandra was so caught up in her own thoughts she cut the evening short, driving herself home again, wondering when she would be able to see Jonas again to finish their conversation. She certainly hadn't been expecting him to be waiting for her when she got home!

But she would know that dark green Jaguar anywhere, and she glanced warily over at the house as she locked her own car before going inside. Obviously Jonas had decided they should finish this conversation tonight!

Jean looked at her with raised brows as she entered the house. 'Mr Hunter is in the sitting-room,' she said ruefully; obviously she hadn't had any choice about letting him wait in there for Cassandra to come home!

'Thanks, Jean.' Cassandra squeezed her arm reassuringly, leaving her bag on the hall table to go through to the sitting-room, straightening her back defensively as she entered.

Jonas stood beside the unlit fireplace, watching her with narrowed eyes as she came in and quietly closed the door behind her. 'Where the hell have you been?' he rasped accusingly.

She gasped at his direct attack. 'I don't think that's any of your——'

'You knew damn well I had assumed you would be at your mother's this evening,' he bit out impatiently.

She shook her head. 'I didn't say I would be,' she reasoned, the two of them facing each other like adversaries across the width of the fireplace.

The perfectly tailored black dinner-suit and snowy white shirt Jonas wore did little to hide the fact that these trappings of civilisation were merely that—a veneer of sophistication that did little to hide the contempt he felt for the polite conventions that meant he had to dress this way to go to dinner at her mother's house.

'No, you didn't say that,' he accepted harshly. 'But you knew I thought it anyway.'

What he thought and what was actually fact were two entirely different things! 'What do you want, Jonas?' she sighed wearily.

'I wanted to finish our earlier conversation,' he ground out impatiently. 'But now I want to know where you were and who you were with this evening.'

Cassandra frowned. 'I don't think that's any of your business,' she repeated, this time actually being allowed to finish the statement!

'Young Grey, I suppose,' he grated, his gaze narrowed on her speculatively. 'Oh, yes, Cassandra, I've heard the rumours of your affair with him.' His mouth twisted contemptuously.

'My what?' she gasped incredulously. 'I'm not having an affair with Simeon!' she protested irritably. 'He and I are friends——'

'You go out together,' Jonas accused.

'Well—yes,' she acknowledged, colour entering her cheeks. 'But as friends. Not that I can see what it has to do with you anyway——'

'You're my brother's widow, the mother of my niece, of course it interests me what men you have in your life——'

'I don't have "men" in my life,' Cassandra protested heatedly. 'Only Simeon. And he——'

'"Only Simeon",' Jonas echoed tauntingly. 'What is it, Cassandra? Is he no danger because his tastes don't run to women?'

'Simeon has a normal interest in women as far as I know,' she defended, indignant on his behalf; just because Simeon was involved in the fashion business didn't mean he was automatically homosexual.

'As far as you know,' Jonas repeated softly, moving in that stealthy way of his now, suddenly standing very close to her. 'Hasn't he tried to make love to you yet?' he challenged.

She swallowed hard, her cheeks feeling very warm now. 'Of course he hasn't!' she snapped, wishing he wouldn't stand so close to her; she was starting to feel very hot indeed, all over!

Jonas's hand came up to cup one side of her heated face, his eyes narrowed on her widely distressed ones. 'Why don't I believe you?' he murmured softly. 'Possibly because of the passion I see here.' His thumb-pad moved caressingly close to her wide golden eyes. 'And the promise I can feel here.' That thumb moved over her bottom lip now. 'And the desire that pulses here.' His hand moved down to the hollows of her throat, gently caressing still. 'I was right about this dress, Cassandra,' he told her softly, looking down at her body sheathed in the gold-coloured gown. 'You do look like a high priestess in it.'

He was standing so close to her now that Cassandra could feel the heat of his body, and the touch of that marauding hand was doing strange things to her limbs; she was having difficulty standing up! She swayed slightly towards him, and as she did so she saw the light of triumph in his eyes, starting to pull back as she did so.

But it was too late; Jonas had already thrust her away from him, looking at her coldly now. 'No,' he rasped harshly, 'I don't believe you at all, Cassandra.' He looked at her contemptuously. 'You and Charles must have made a great pair, he so self-centred and you so glad to give him what he wanted as long as you got what you wanted in return!'

'Get out,' Cassandra choked. 'Get out of my house.' It was still hers—just!

Jonas's mouth twisted. 'Quite like old times!' He taunted, reminding her of the fact that she had thrown him out the first time he had come here too. 'Oh, I'm going, Cassandra, don't worry. I had wanted to talk to you again before I left for the States in the morning but——'

'You're going to America tomorrow?' Cassandra gasped incredulously; he had given no indication of that earlier today.

His eyes narrowed. 'Is there some problem with that?'

'Well, no... But——'

'Good,' he accepted with brisk dismissal. 'We can talk again when I get back.'

Cassandra hurried after him as he strode over to the door. 'But——'

'Yes, Cassandra?' He turned so sharply that she almost walked into him. She looked up into the hard

coldness of his face, shivering slightly at the cruelty she
could see there; he knew exactly what he was doing, was
well aware of how worried she was about the conversation they had had earlier. Damn him!

'Nothing,' she told him through gritted teeth. 'It can
wait until you get back.'

His mouth twisted into a humourless smile. 'It will
have to—won't it...?'

Cassandra stood alone in the sitting-room long after
he had gone, shivering in spite of the warmth of the
house. And while she was upset about Jonas's cruel determination not to finish their earlier conversation she
was more disturbed by the way she had seemed to respond to him, no matter how briefly...

Jonas was in New York all of the following week, and
the longer he was away, the more agitated Cassandra
became. She desperately needed to know what he had
found out during that company audit. And despite the
need to keep her own flagging business going, having to
complete her spring designs before the New Year, it was
her work that suffered the most with the upset of waiting
for Jonas's return. So much so that when Bethany was
invited out by her grandmother on the Sunday for a visit
to the zoo Cassandra telephoned Simeon and asked if
he would mind coming over to the house and working
with her there for the day.

A working Sunday lunch, the remnants of their picnic-
style meal still on the small coffee-table over by the armchair, their half-empty wine glasses left untouched, the
fire glowing warm and inviting—it all looked extremely
warm and cosy, Cassandra realised ruefully as she

straightened to rub a soothing hand over her aching nape, where she had been bent over the sketches all afternoon.

Which was exactly the conclusion Jonas drew too, she realised with extreme irritation, when he arrived a short time later!

After waiting a week to see him, her nerves strung out to breaking-point, when the moment did finally arrive, it was, she was sure, after their conversation concerning Simeon a week ago, in what Jonas considered a compromising situation; there was no mistaking the harsh criticism in that hard black gaze as it raked over her with merciless judgement!

If she had known he was back, perhaps she wouldn't have invited Simeon here today. And then perhaps she would! This was her home, she could behave as she liked in the privacy of it. Jonas was the intruder here.

When she had heard Jean answer the ring of the doorbell, closely followed by Bethany's excited chatter, Cassandra had known that work was over for the day, shooting Simeon a rueful smile as he came to the same conclusion and began to gather the things together that they had spread over the floor so that they could work more easily.

The door burst open and Bethany rushed in to tell her all about the animals she had seen, Cassandra not realising for several minutes of Bethany's chatter that a man had followed her to stand in the doorway—a man who surveyed the intimacy of the scene he had walked in on with a calculating narrowing of his coal-black eyes! By the time Cassandra had realised it was Jonas who had brought Bethany home, and not Joy and Colin as her mother had told her it probably would be, Jonas had already made his assessment of the situation he had interrupted, and was looking at her with accusing contempt.

To make matters worse, Simeon had seen that narrow-eyed look too, glancing uncomfortably at Cassandra as he tried to gauge her reaction to the other man's obvious anger at finding them here together. Cassandra could have screamed at how guilty Simeon suddenly looked, at the way he was acting like a man 'caught in the act', his movements agitated now as he hastened to clear away.

God, so much for her having told Jonas his accusations concerning Simeon and herself were false ones; even *she* was starting to feel guilty, and she had nothing to feel guilty about!

She slowly released Bethany as her daughter paused for breath in her narrative, standing up herself now, very aware, in the face of Jonas's neat appearance in fitted black trousers and cobalt-blue sweater, of her own dishevelled appearance. Her denims and jumper were far from new, and she had a habit, when she was working, of pushing her hair haphazardly back from her face; from the expression on Jonas's face as he took in her appearance as she stood up he was imagining someone else's fingers completely having caressed the dark cascade of her ebony hair!

'Jonas,' she greeted him much more lightly than she felt. 'I didn't realise you were back.' The last was as much an accusation as a statement; he must know she had been wanting to speak to him all week!

'Obviously,' he rasped with an acknowledging inclination of his head, giving Simeon a cold glare.

Cassandra sighed wearily as she saw how worried the younger man was looking now. 'It's very kind of you to have brought Bethany home for me,' she added dismissively, 'although I had been expecting Joy and Colin to do that.' And she was curious to know at what juncture during the day Jonas had joined her family so that he had been in a position to bring Bethany home at all. God knew what construction Joy would put on that little fact!

Jonas shrugged unconcernedly, strolling further into the room, completely in command of the situation—even though he must know Cassandra's feelings towards him were ambivalent to say the least. 'I went to your mother's to see Colin about something, and when I realised Joy and Colin have an appointment to see the vicar later this evening, obviously concerning the wedding arrangements, it seemed only logical I should be the one to drive Bethany home,' he explained.

Logical. Methodical. Calculated. Cold! All of those adequately described this man.

Cassandra gave an involuntary shiver, stiffening her shoulders in what she knew was a defensive way. 'Well, it was very nice of you to do so——'

'I've invited Uncle Jonas to stay for tea,' Bethany piped up happily, her hand sliding conspiratorially into her uncle's as she smiled up at him adoringly.

Cassandra looked down at her daughter in dismay. In the past she had always found pleasure in the fact that her daughter was so outgoing; Bethany's friends from school seeming endless, a constant stream of them coming to the house for tea since Bethany had started at the school in September. But Jonas was hardly a schoolfriend of Bethany's, and Cassandra couldn't exactly say she was pleased at this deepening closeness between the two of them. Since Jonas was only a distant, nominal male in her daughter's life, Cassandra could cope with his occasional visits, but she knew he must have returned from the States some time over the weekend—and one of the first things he seemed to have done was spend time with Bethany. And Cassandra didn't like it, not one little bit.

'Unless we're too late...?' Jonas looked pointedly at the debris left on the table from the snack lunch Cassandra and Simeon had enjoyed together earlier. And which, Cassandra was sure he realised, had to have been there some time; the bread was starting to curl up at the edges, for goodness' sake! He was just being bloody-minded again.

'I'll have Jean clear that away.' She rang for the other woman, Jean knowing from experience that she had to just leave Cassandra when she was working, which was why she hadn't cleared away earlier. Cassandra turned to Simeon. 'Would you like to join us for tea too?' Even as she made the request he met the pleading in her eyes with apology—and request it certainly was; she didn't want to be left alone here with the rapier-tongued Jonas. Not that she could blame Simeon for his defection; given the choice she would have joined him and fled too!

'I'm afraid I already have an appointment this evening,' Simeon refused with obvious relief for this previously made engagement—although Cassandra was sure he would have invented one if he hadn't had one! 'Mr Hunter.' He nodded his parting to the other man, stepping forward to give Cassandra the customary kiss on the cheek—and then thinking better of it as hard black eyes narrowed ominously, a slight flush to his boyish cheeks now as he gave Cassandra a nervously apologetic smile. 'Cassandra. Bethany.' He fled out into the hallway after the last, the firm click of the front door closing seconds later confirming his departure.

'"Mr Hunter",' Jonas repeated with cold derision. 'Are all your lovers as polite to your relatives?'

Cassandra gasped as he once again caught her off guard with the intimacy of his attack. But at the same time she was very aware of the listening Bethany—and of how her daughter loved to relate what she had overheard to other people!

'I told you, Simeon isn't my lover!' she hissed with a pointed look in Bethany's direction. 'And you aren't a relative of mine,' she added firmly.

'No?' Dark brows rose. 'I'm Bethany's uncle, so I must be related to you too.'

Half-brothers of dead husbands didn't count. If the half-brother had been anyone other than Jonas, then he might have done, but it was him, and there was nothing she could do to erase the antagonism she felt towards him every time they met. In fact, she was sure it was an antagonism he deliberately nurtured. Quite why she had no idea.

With Charles dead, her left as his widow, Jonas his half-brother, they should really have been drawn together in the grief of having lost Charles so suddenly. But Jonas still seemed to harbour some past resentment towards Charles which prevented him from feeling any other emotion towards him—or the woman Charles had married!

Oh, Jonas had returned to England to take over the company, but she really knew little about him. Peter, Charles's and Jonas's father, had little to say about his younger son when Cassandra visited him with Bethany, and she somehow didn't think the rift that had existed between them before Jonas left England all those years ago had been healed either.

Of course Peter was getting old now, well into his seventies, becoming frailer all the time, spending most of his time in seclusion at his Berkshire home, increasingly so since Charles's death. But surely Peter's advanced years and declining health were added reasons why he and Jonas should now try to sort out their differences? It was——

'Mummy, what's a lover?' Bethany's puzzled voice effectively cut into her thoughts.

'If you don't understand, ask,' Cassandra had always told her daughter—and now wished she hadn't! 'Why don't you ask Uncle Jonas to explain, darling?' she suggested brightly, having thankfully spotted Jean waiting patiently in the doorway after having come in answer to her ring. 'While I go and organise tea with Jean.' She shot Jonas a smugly triumphant smile before sweeping out of the room and closing the door firmly behind her, uncaring if her actions looked slightly childish; Jonas had brought the subject up—he could deal with it!

Jean raised blonde brows peppered with grey. 'What was all that about?'

'Don't ask!' Cassandra squeezed the other woman's arm in gratitude for her timely rescue.

'I had a feeling you might say that.' Jean gave a rueful chuckle. 'Tea for three, I gather?'

Cassandra pulled a face. 'It appears that we have a guest, yes.'

Jonas didn't exactly join them for tea; he joined Bethany. Cassandra might just as well not have been there for all the notice he took of her as the toasted tea-cakes and muffins, both dripping with butter, fast disappeared, followed by huge chunks of Jean's fruit-cake.

What Jonas had told Bethany in answer to her question about 'a lover' Cassandra didn't enquire, but Bethany seemed satisfied, whatever it had been!

But still Jonas made no effort to leave once tea had been eaten and cleared away, offering to help bath Bethany when the time came, an offer it would have looked churlish to refuse. Not that Cassandra would have minded looking churlish where this man was concerned, but once again Bethany was involved, and once the suggestion had been made her daughter was all for it, especially after Jonas had suggested they play battle-ships among the bubbles in the jacuzzi. Cassandra gave up any idea of diverting her daughter after that!

She was starting to feel as if her life here with Bethany was being invaded, and not slowly either; Jonas was doing this the way he did everything, head-on, without a care as to whose feelings he might be trampling on— certainly not Cassandra's! And Cassandra would be lying, to herself as much as anyone else, if she didn't admit she felt slightly hurt by Bethany's easy defection to this man she hadn't even known until nine months ago. She even had to stand by tonight while Jonas read Bethany her bedtime story, a nightly ritual mother and daughter had always shared together, even when Charles was alive. Cassandra had always made a point, no matter

how busy she was, or where they happened to be, of
putting Bethany to bed herself and reading her the
bedtime story.

But not tonight. Tonight Jonas was given that honour.
And feeling superfluous—as well as slightly hurt,
although she couldn't blame Bethany, for she knew the
little girl was enjoying this male attention—Cassandra
left them to it.

How odd. It was such a little thing, just a bedtime
story before Bethany snuggled down in her bed for the
night, and yet Cassandra felt bereft at being denied this
enjoyable routine for the first time since her daughter
had been born. Utterly ridiculous to feel this way,
Cassandra knew as she sat down dejectedly on her own
bed. Was she becoming selfish where Bethany was concerned, over-protective, possessive...? She hadn't
thought so, and yet——

She heard Jonas leave Bethany's bedroom and go
downstairs, realised she should go down and join him,
but knowing she wasn't ready to do so yet. She was still
disturbed by her own reaction, by those feelings of
rejection.

It didn't help to learn, when she checked in on Bethany
a few minutes later on her way downstairs, that her
daughter had enjoyed the change in story-teller
immensely!

'Uncle Jonas is wonderful, isn't he, Mummy?' Bethany
murmured sleepily, her eyes aglow, not really expecting
an answer—— Which was just as well, because
Cassandra couldn't think of a single complimentary thing
to say about the man!

And so she said nothing, just smiling gently, Bethany falling asleep even as Cassandra sat watching her, the little girl absolutely worn out by her busy day.

How innocent and untroubled Bethany looked in sleep, totally safe and secure in her own little world—thank God. It could all have turned out so differently, Cassandra knew, after they had lost Charles so suddenly, and she was gratefull beyond belief that, although Bethany missed her father, there didn't seem to be any emotional repercussions on Bethany from his death. Except this growing affection Bethany was developing for Jonas!

It came as something of a shock to Cassandra to discover, when she finally made her way down to her little sitting-room, that Jonas had fallen asleep in there! And he looked far from innocent and untroubled in the same state!

Seeming to have fallen back against the sofa, having drifted off to sleep in spite of himself, the harshness was still there in the hardness of his cheeks and jaw, dark lashes fanned down over those piercing black eyes behind the glasses he wore again today, a vulnerability that on any other man would have been boyishly endearing. Not on Jonas. The inward power that was this man still emanated from him, giving the impression that he would open his eyes at any moment and pin her to the spot with that lethal black gaze.

And at that moment he did exactly that!

Cassandra was held captive as she hesitated in the doorway, like a butterfly held on a pin, Jonas's narrowed gaze fixed on her as he slowly stretched, flexing his limbs from the uncomfortable position he had been in.

Why couldn't he be like other people, she fumed inwardly, and wake up slightly disorientated by his surroundings, and feel vulnerable because of that? What a stupid question, she berated herself even as she thought of it; Jonas didn't have a vulnerable bone in his body!

'Sorry about that,' he drawled without any real apology, sitting forward forcibly. 'Jet lag,' he shrugged. 'I only arrived back from the States early this morning.'

And he had thundered straight back into their lives, Cassandra realised with a frown. Why?

'I thought perhaps you might want to see me,' Jonas told her mockingly, eyes narrowed.

Yes, of course she did, but on her terms, not when she was still feeling slightly off-balance about her resentment concerning his closeness to Bethany. She wanted to sit down as a business partner and discuss what was, after all, a business matter, not deal with this now, when she still felt vulnerable in her position as Bethany's mother, let alone this man's business equal!

'As it happens,' he continued softly, not seeming at all bothered that she had so far made no response to his remarks, 'I wanted to see you too.'

She eyed him warily. 'You did?'

'Yes,' he confirmed huskily, his mouth twisting derisively at the sudden tension that emanated from her. 'Why don't you come into the room and close the door, Cassandra?' he suggested quietly, not having moved from his sitting position on the sofa, and yet seeming to dominate the room with his presence anyway. 'What I have to say is private. Very private,' he repeated softly.

Like a spider setting a trap for the unsuspecting fly. But she wasn't completely unsuspecting, had been warned, she knew, by Jonas himself, over a week ago. And yet still she felt at a disadvantage against this man, knowing he was capable of using any leverage he chose to achieve what he wanted.

But there was no way she could have even guessed what it was he did want!

CHAPTER FOUR

CASSANDRA stared at him with wide, horrified eyes. 'Would—would you repeat that? Please...' she added as a numbed afterthought. She couldn't, just couldn't have heard him right the first time!

Jonas looked mildly amused by her response. 'I said, I want you to marry me,' he repeated calmly.

She had heard him right the first time! Why? was her next thought. Jonas despised her, had made his opinion of her more than plain from the beginning; he couldn't possibly want her as his own wife when he had such contempt for her for marrying the brother he had despised. And yet that was exactly what he had said; he wanted her to marry him.

Thank God she had closed the sitting-room door now; she would have hated an unsuspecting Jean to have been passing the room and overheard Jonas's remark, or, even worse, Bethany, come downstairs in search of that glass of water she occasionally delayed bedtime with!

Cassandra looked frowningly across the room at Jonas now, trying to guess from his expression what he could possibly be thinking of. She should have known better; Jonas gave nothing of his thoughts away that he didn't want people to know! And at this moment in time he didn't want her to know anything other than what he told her, his expression enquiring as she continued to stare at him, coal-black eyes meeting her searching gaze with cool disdain. Nothing. And yet she knew he had just said he wanted to marry her...

It was like a nightmare, but she knew, as Jonas continued to look at her with that steadily unnerving intent, that it was a nightmare she wasn't going to wake up from!

She drew in a ragged breath to her starved lungs, her hands tightly clenched together in front of her—the latter so that Jonas shouldn't see how badly they were trembling. Although, knowing Jonas, he probably knew exactly what effect his words had had on her.

'Why?' was all she could finally manage to say.

'Ah, Cassandra.' To her surprise his smile held pleasure. 'I knew I could rely on you not to disappoint me!'

Her frown deepened; she couldn't begin to know what this man was talking about! Perhaps all of this was just a bad reaction to jet lag on his part, she thought hopefully. And then her hopes were dashed again as she remembered he had been perfectly lucid when he arrived. But he had fallen asleep since then, so perhaps——

'No false cries of, "Oh, Jonas, this is so sudden",' he rasped with obvious derision. 'Or, "Oh, Jonas, I didn't know you cared!"' His mouth twisted harshly.

It was sudden, but as she knew only too well that he didn't care... 'I repeat, Jonas, why?' She still eyed him warily, taking an involuntary step backwards as he stood up, colour darkening her cheeks as he saw the movement and raised mocking brows.

He was smiling again now, but it was still a smile that unnerved. 'Because, my dear Cassandra——'

'I'm not your dear anything!' she cut in heatedly, stung by his obvious derision.

'No,' he acknowledged hardly, all humour fading now. 'But you will be my wife. You see,' he continued firmly as she would have protested once again, 'you have something I want. But equally I have something you want.'

She doubted that immensely! And yet... He looked so confident, so sure of himself. She tensed warily once again, sensing there was so much more to come.

'The thing is, Cassandra...' he spoke almost conversationally now, his hands in his trouser pockets as he rocked slowly backwards and forwards on his heels '...twenty-five per cent of Hunter and Kyle shares just isn't enough to run the company effectively.' He looked at her challengingly as she at first frowned, and then gasped in astonishment, as she realised exactly what he was saying. The only thing he could possibly want from her to enable him to have more control over Hunter and Kyle was her shares—the ten per cent left to her by her father! But if that were so, what could he possibly have that she would want from——? Oh, God, no, she inwardly groaned, as she realised exactly what exchange he was offering her. It had to be that!

'Yes, Cassandra.' Jonas smiled now, not unpleasantly; after all, he had no reason to be nasty—he was the man who knew he held all the aces up his sleeve! 'The little matter of the audit I've just had done of the company. And we both know what the accountants found—don't we?' he prompted softly.

Cassandra looked at him searchingly, wondering just how much he knew. Everything, from the triumphant glitter in those night-dark eyes.

She had been so numbed after Charles's death so soon after her father's, her fashion business falling more and more into debt, until she wasn't sure how much longer she could go on, that she hadn't given a thought to the problem that dogged Hunter and Kyle, and by the time she had realised exactly what a catastrophe had befallen them all Jonas was in charge, and as the days and then weeks passed, and he made no mention of—of what had been going on she had thought Charles must have been wrong about the seriousness of the problem after all. If he hadn't, Jonas would surely have discovered it and demanded to know exactly what had been happening at Hunter and Kyle during the year before the two partners' deaths.

That's what she had thought. Until a week ago. When Jonas first mentioned that audit to her. But this was family, and surely Jonas realised that any scandal that came out about the company would affect them all...?

But she knew, even as she looked pleadingly at the harshness of his face, that Jonas knew exactly how much of company funds had been diverted into another, private company, for the personal use of one of its partners. She could also see from the hard lack of sympathy in his expression that he now intended exacting his pound of flesh for the knowledge, down to the last ounce—or share!

She moistened suddenly dry lips. 'How did they find out?' Was that really her voice, that husky quaver that seemed to border on tears?

'It was very cleverly done, I grant you. I can even admire the way in which it was achieved.' He gave an acknowledging inclination of his head. 'A maze within a maze. Which was why I hadn't realised exactly what was going on long ago. Maybe I should have realised;

after all, I got my business grounding in the toughest market in the world, in New York, where money is everything, and there are no gentlemen,' he said grimly.

No one could ever accuse him of being that, Cassandra inwardly agreed.

'But I'm completely aware of the facts now,' he continued harshly. 'Feel confident about coming to you and confronting you with your father's embezzling of company funds for his own personal use,' he said disgustedly.

Cassandra stared at him, all the colour draining from her face once again.

'Yes.' Jonas's mouth twisted at her obvious reaction. 'It isn't very pleasant when you say it out loud, is it?' he dismissed hardly. 'But you can see why I think it only fair, in the circumstances, that your father's ten per cent of the company should return to a Hunter——'

'I'm a Hunter,' she cut in sharply, her thoughts racing at the things he was saying.

Jonas looked at her coldly. 'At the moment, yes, and if you marry me, you'll remain so,' he rasped. 'But if you married someone like that young puppy you've been seeing, the one I found you with here this afternoon——'

'I told you,' she defended heatedly, 'my friendship with Simeon is a platonic one; there is no relationship.' There had been no one else in her life of a romantic nature from the day she started going out with Charles over five years ago. There certainly hadn't been any other men for her since his death ten months ago.

Jonas nodded grimly. 'And I'm sure we'll *work* just as well together,' he drawled disparagingly, raising dark brows as she gave a scornful snort at the claim. 'You don't think so?' he challenged softly, advancing across the room towards her on that soft tread of his that was so surprising for such a large man.

Six feet three, one hundred and eighty pounds, and he moved with all the stealthy grace of a jungle cat—which was precisely what he was, if his claim about New York was true!

And she was mentally burbling—she shouldn't just be standing here like a mesmerised rabbit waiting to become his prey! Too late, she realised when Jonas pulled her effortlessly up against him, his arms like steel bands as the movement of his head lowering towards hers cut out all the light in the room and left her only darkness.

His mouth claiming hers was like an electric shock, seeming to reach every nerve-ending in her body, his lips moving possessively against hers now as she would have tried to pull away, as if he was only claiming an owner-ship he already knew he had.

Cassandra's head swam at the onslaught of emotions that swamped her, swaying unsteadily against him, until his arms clamped more tightly about her, moulding the length of her body to his; every hard muscle and sinew imprinted against her much softer curves, the heat of his body burning her flesh even through the jumper she wore. But he controlled by mere strength alone, she in-wardly screamed, unable to break the kiss as one of his hands became entangled in the hair at her nape, holding her captive against him while his lips plundered hers again and again.

As if aware of her mute accusation, Jonas suddenly lifted his head to look down into her flushed face, her

eyes feverish with the painful humiliation of being sub-
jected to his will in this way, a nerve pulsing wildly in
the hardness of his jaw as he continued to look at her.

Her eyes widened in panic as his head lowered towards hers once again, prepared for his savagery this
time, but completely lost as his lips didn't devour but
moved gently against hers, Jonas like a man sipping from
a rare wine, the length of his hands gently cradling either
side of her face now as he sipped again and again, slowly
slaking his thirst. And, to her everlasting shame,
Cassandra felt a similar thirst within herself, a burning
ache she had thought she would never know again...

As if he was perfectly aware of that weakness, Jonas
raised his head at that moment, his gaze triumphant as
he put her firmly away from him. 'We *work* very well
together,' he drawled his satisfaction of the fact, seeming
unaffected by the passion that had flared so briefly between them.

Or had it? Had Jonas been even briefly affected by
those languorous kisses, or had he just been proving to
her that she could know passion in his arms?

Cassandra turned away with a deep sob of self-disgust.
They didn't *work* at all, she told herself vehemently. No
one had held her since Charles had died, not really held
her. Oh, there had been the little consolatory pats on
the back or on her hand, from people who felt sorry for
her loss, but no one had actually taken her in his or her
arms and hugged her. And she hadn't become removed
from the need for human warmth and comfort as this
man seemed to have over the years; rather she had
hungered for that physical contact that had once been
such a part of her life. Only last week she had felt that

same need for someone to hold her as she fretted about whether or not she was doing the right things for Bethany, had——

Oh, God, shut up, Cassandra, she admonished herself. She had responded to Jonas—Jonas, a man she had every reason to fear! Was she so desperate for physical warmth that she had been reduced to that?

'Don't knock good old-fashioned lust, Cassandra,' Jonas taunted now as he saw that look of self-loathing on her face. 'It's probably all we'll have going for us once we're married,' he added harshly.

'I don't want to marry you,' she choked; now, more than ever, she didn't want that, badly needing to cry at what she considered was a betrayal of herself with this man, but knowing she dared not show any more signs of weakness to Jonas. She had no doubt the cynical Jonas would consider tears the ultimate in feminine wiles—and that he would despise her even more than he already did for resorting to them.

'I'm well aware of that,' he dismissed as he moved away, hands back in his trouser pockets. 'I don't particularly want a wife either——'

'Then——'

'But I do want those shares, Cassandra,' he continued hardly, his expression grim now. 'I also want to be in a position to secure the future of my niece.'

'Bethany...?' Cassandra frowned at him.

'Yes—Bethany,' he said grimly. 'I don't think you are capable of offering her security any longer. Are you?'

He knew. Had somehow found out just how desperately in debt her business had become. How had he found out? God, the same way he found out everything else, she mentally berated herself; he was Jonas Hunter, wasn't he?

'And I'm not about to let you use your power over Bethany's shares to bail yourself—or your business—out of the mess it's in,' he told her grimly.

He actually believed she would somehow try to deprive Bethany of the shares left to her by Charles; it was too ridiculous for words! And yet she could see from the uncompromising set of Jonas's mouth that he really did believe she was capable of doing that to her own daughter. What a family he thought them to be—her father an embezzler from his own company, she not above stealing from her own child when it transpired that the husband she had married only for his money—according to Jonas!—hadn't left those shares to her and so left her in a position to help her ailing company!

It would be laughable if it didn't all have such serious repercussions.

Jonas said, 'Your father wasn't averse to stealing from his own partner and son-in-law, let alone the other shareholders, so why shouldn't you——?'

'That's enough!' Cassandra told him coldly, golden eyes as hard as the metal they resembled, her hands clenched into fists at her sides. 'Whatever you may think of me, I know I would never do something like that to Bethany.' She shook her head, wishing she could dismiss his accusations towards her father as easily. But if she did, what then? It was that uncertainty that kept her silent on that subject. But if she remained silent this man was demanding she marry him . . . !

She looked at Jonas now, fear in her heart at the harshness that was such a fundamental part of him, knowing that to marry him would be like selling her soul to the devil—at his price!

How could she marry him?

How could she not?

Jonas wasn't actually giving her a choice, not an acceptable one, at least. It was a straightforward exchange as far as he was concerned—marriage to him, with her ten per cent of Hunter and Kyle to be handed over to him, in return for his silence, and providing for Bethany's future, something that had, she had to admit, been troubling her deeply since she had realised just how serious things were financially. A lot of it, she knew, was due to Charles, and his philosophy that tomorrow could take care of itself. There was no money left to pay for anything! All she had left to sell was her shares. And this man wanted those in return for his silence concerning that diversion of company funds. But would his silence be enough?

She put her head back challengingly, disturbed to find he had been watching her with those piercing black eyes as those thoughts flittered and warred in her mind. 'How is my marrying you going to make any difference to those—discrepancies you've discovered in company funds?' She frowned warily. 'I would, surely, only be buying one man's silence,' she added with deliberate insult for all the times he had done the same thing to her.

'If the money your father—borrowed——' his mouth twisted disgustedly ' —is returned to the company before the end of the year, no one will be any the wiser, and the other shareholders will never have to know what was going on.'

Cassandra's frown deepened. 'Are you saying—you could do that?'

He looked at her mockingly. 'Does knowing I'm that wealthy make it easier for you to make up your mind about marrying me?' he taunted.

'No!' she snapped abruptly. 'I was just—surprised,' she admitted resentfully, having no idea he was that wealthy in his own right. It made no difference whatsoever to whether or not she married him!

He shrugged dismissively. 'I can easily cover the—discrepancy.'

He didn't add any more, nothing at all about the way he had made his money, although it was obvious he must have come by his wealth since going to America all those years ago; according to Charles, when Jonas had walked out on the family, he had taken nothing with him but a suitcase and his plane ticket. Cassandra was prepared to believe, from what she had come to know of Jonas, that he had made his money through white slave-trading! Although he had told her himself there were no gentlemen successfully in business in New York—so Jonas should have been very successful indeed!

She knew how much money the company was short, had known, with the way things were with her own company, that she could nowhere near cover the loss, otherwise she would have done it long before now—long before Jonas could fling such an insulting proposal of marriage at her!

'If I'm really the mercenary little bitch you seem to think I am,' she rasped, 'why on earth should it matter to me one way or the other if you discredit my father in the way you're proposing?' She was trying to call his bluff—and maybe if her voice hadn't broken emotionally she might have stood a chance of succeeding. Although she doubted it! She felt like a poor bird that had been put into a cage, and the door was slowly, oh, so slowly, closing behind her...

Jonas's mouth twisted confidently. 'A scandal like this one could rock the company very badly.'

'So?' Cassandra challenged with brave defiance—at least trying to beat her wings against the cage that was closing in around her, no matter how futile it was.

He shrugged, still smiling that confident smile that was so unnerving. 'Companies have been known to crumble for less. As I've just told you, I'm wealthy enough in my own right for it not to bother me. I'll just pack up my bags and return to the States, but your family, and you, would collapse like a pack of cards,' he concluded dismissively.

He had made his point, crystal-clear. 'And Bethany; what would happen to her?' After all, he had made it obvious he thought she would try to cheat her own child; what good would he be doing Bethany if he ruined the company and there was no inheritance for her, especially when her mother's company was on the point of collapse too?

His mouth tightened at the gibe. 'I would take care of Bethany,' he ground out savagely. 'In my own way. On my own terms,' he added hardly.

Cassandra felt a shiver of apprehension down her spine, not even wanting to contemplate what his 'terms' would be. What she did know, didn't doubt for a moment, was that Jonas was more than capable of carrying out his threat.

She swallowed hard. 'You were wrong about me, Jonas—— Oh, yes, you were,' she insisted heavily at his derisive snort. 'And about so many more things than I could ever hope to convince you of. But they weren't what I was talking about when I said you were wrong about me.' She straightened determinedly, feeling as if she had a heavy weight on her shoulders that was slowly trying to drag her down. 'I am going to say "this is so sudden, Jonas",' she sighed wearily, running a not quite steady hand across her furrowed brow. 'I need time to— to think about—all that you've said to me today.'

'Time to consider your options?' he scorned—knowing she couldn't have any, or she would have used them by now!

'Yes,' Cassandra said defensively, tears clouding her vision at how vulnerable she felt.

Damn Charles, for leaving her like this, for not providing for his daughter at least! Oh, God, she groaned inwardly, what good was blaming Charles going to do? He was dead; she was the one who would have to take care of Bethany now. But she couldn't just meekly agree to marry Jonas, had to at least think about what she would be letting herself in for by becoming his wife.

His eyes were narrowed, his expression implacable. 'How much time?'

As much time as it took, she wanted to scream at him! This was the rest of her life they were talking about here. She hadn't expected it to be ecstatically happy, but she had at least thought she would be left in peace to enjoy Bethany and her career. Her career had already gone, and if she married Jonas he would infiltrate every part of her life with his dominating presence, wouldn't allow her any peace at all with his constantly mocking remarks. But, at the same time, what choice did she have...?

She might know she was being inescapably drawn into a living nightmare, but she certainly didn't have to leap into it without at least trying to find other options first!

'I'm not sure,' she dismissed awkwardly, having trouble thinking at all at the moment. 'At least until after Christmas——'

'I'll give you until Christmas Eve to give me your answer,' Jonas cut in determinedly. 'I want to announce our engagement at Christmas, and the wedding to take place by special licence by the New Year——'

'So soon?' she gasped, eyes wide with horror. A week—he was only giving her a week to decide on the rest of her life, two weeks before she would have to become his wife!

His mouth twisted as he easily read her emotion. 'A big society wedding wouldn't be appropriate in the circumstances—thank God! And if I straighten out the company accounts before we're actually married you may just decide to call off the wedding in the hope that I won't do anything about those discrepancies then!' he said knowingly.

Colour flooded her cheeks at the ease with which he was able to read her thoughts; she had frantically been searching for some way she could agree to his proposal and then delay things until she could find a way out of this mess. Although she already knew there wasn't a way; hadn't she been having the same desperate thoughts about repaying that money for almost a year now, growing angry with Charles once the shock of his death had worn off? It might have been all too easy to love the charmingly irresponsible man he was, but it wasn't helping to provide for Bethany and herself now. And she knew she just didn't have the resources to do it herself either.

And this man did...

The first she had learnt of the misappropriation of funds from Hunter and Kyle had been when Charles told her of it shortly after her father's death. She had been dumbfounded, totally at a loss to know what to do, but, with his usual optimism, Charles had been confident that they could weather the storm—given time. But he hadn't been given time, had been dead himself two months later. And Cassandra had been living in fear ever since, desperately afraid that Jonas would discover what had been going on, while at the same time knowing someone would have to in the end. There was just too much money involved for it to have passed undetected for much longer...!

Maybe she should have gone to Jonas in the beginning, not let it get to the stage where he could blackmail her like this; she should have appealed to him to help her find some way out of the mess before the other shareholders had to be told. But without Charles beside her, his certainty always that things would work out, she hadn't known what to do. And now it was too late to do anything...

'Charles knew, didn't he?' Jonas suddenly rasped harshly, his narrowed gaze levelled on the paleness of her face. 'My God, of course he knew,' he said in sudden realisation. 'That was what killed him, wasn't it?' he accused incredulously. 'Wasn't it, Cassandra?' he repeated with savage intent, grasping the tops of her arms now as he attempted to shake an answer out of her. 'Answer me, damn you!' He shook her roughly.

His hands were painful on her arms, but in a way she welcomed the pain, the tears that flooded her eyes but remained unshed, blinding her now to the savage anger in his harshly etched face.

Charles had known. Of course Charles had known; how could he not know? He and her father were partners. And they had remained so even after the confession had been made, the two men having come to a decision that they would sort out over the festive holidays what could be done to salvage the loss. In fact, they had been working on it in this very house during the evening before Cassandra's father was killed on his drive home. Cassandra had been numbed by the tragedy, but Charles had been devastated, not knowing where to turn now to look for a way out of the mess. Which was when he had confided in Cassandra. Like a confused little boy, he had come to her to help find a solution, looking for answers she didn't have either.

'Answer me!' Jonas demanded fiercely, black eyes glittering as he shook her once again.

Cassandra looked at him blankly for several seconds. 'Yes,' she finally choked. 'Yes, it was what killed him!' she cried in anguish.

Because she had never doubted it, not for moment; she knew it had to have been the strain that had brought on Charles's heart attack at such a young age.

Jonas's hands dropped away from her arms as if they were burnt, a look of utter disgust on his face as he judged—and found her guilty!—once again.

This man who thought he knew so much . . .

CHAPTER FIVE

'SIMEON never stood a chance, did he?' Joy said knowingly, Cassandra and Bethany having called at the house on Christmas Eve to deliver their presents—and, unknowingly to Bethany, to collect her gifts too so that she had them delivered with her others by Father Christmas in the morning. Marguerite was even now outside supervising the gifts being stowed away in the boot of Cassandra's car.

Unfortunately, Joy hadn't yet left for her evening out with Colin; and Cassandra, although she wished it were otherwise, had no doubts as to what her sister was referring to. She gave a pointed look of warning in Bethany's direction as her daughter occupied herself placing the gifts for her aunt and grandmother under the grandly decorated tree that stood at one end of the elegant sitting-room.

'Perhaps we can discuss this some other time, Joy,' Cassandra suggested firmly.

Her sister gave a derisive smile. 'It's a little late in the day to be *discussing* anything, I would have thought!'

Cassandra gave her a sharply querying look, forgetting Bethany for the moment as she saw her young daughter was busily examining other gifts under the tree now, totally absorbed in what she was doing. 'What do you mean by that?' she softly prompted Joy into an explanation for the enigmatic remark.

Joy drew deeply on the cigarette she was smoking, eyes narrowed speculatively behind the lingering curls of smoke. 'A little bird tells me that Jonas had been casting those lovely dark eyes of his over engagement rings,' she drawled. 'And as you're the only woman he's been seen with recently—almost every night last week, wasn't it...?' She raised mocking brows. 'I can only assume that you must be the lucky lady intended to receive whichever rock he decides upon from the exclusive collection he had delivered for his inspection to his office!'

Jonas had been looking at engagement rings? She wasn't even supposed to give him her answer until this evening; was he so sure of her that he had the arrogance to have already chosen a ring for her? Cassandra knew he was—on both counts! And Joy was absolutely right about the amount of time Jonas had spent at her home this last week—although she had no intention of asking her sister how she could possibly have known that; Joy would just find it amusing that she should be so uptight about her knowing!

The truth of the matter was that a lot of the time Jonas had spent with them this last week had actually been concentrated on Bethany, as he became closer and closer emotionally to the child. He had come to the house straight from the office most evenings, consequently having his evening meal with the two of them too. In fact, the night before last, Jean had actually asked him before he left for the evening if she was to expect him for a meal the next night! Not that Cassandra blamed her housekeeper for wanting to know; it wasn't easy for the other woman to keep preparing meals that could cater for a third person, if need be. The proof that it paid to

know in advance was borne out by the especially sumptuous meal Jean had prepared for them all last night!

But that didn't mean that Cassandra accepted Jonas's
arrogance in assuming he had some sort of right to eat
with them every evening! Just as it was equally obvious
that Jonas didn't give a damn what she thought—he was
going to do it anyway!

She hated the insidious way he was taking over her
life, knew that if she married him she was going to deeply
resent his totally dominating presence in her life. If she
married him! Good God, they both knew she had no
choice but to marry him, that her refusal to give him
his answer until the time she had stated was only de-
laying the inevitable; she felt like a fish floundering on
the end of a hook, and Jonas was slowly but assuredly
reeling in the line. Nevertheless, she kept fighting until
the last possible moment...

And she couldn't for the life of her understand how
Joy could describe Jonas as having 'lovely dark eyes';
they always seemed coldly determined to her, totally
lacking in warmth!

'I don't know where you got your information from,
Joy,' she began with rueful dismissal. 'But——'

'A very reliable source, believe me,' Joy cut in with
a confident smile.

Cassandra did believe her, and could only assume that
Jonas had actually had the rings brought to the offices
of Hunter and Kyle for him to look at, as Joy had
claimed he had; he was just arrogant enough to demand
such a personal service from any exclusive jeweller's he
felt inclined to use! And no doubt Colin, knowing exactly

what was going on, had taken great delight in telling Joy all about it.

'If you've been worrying about how far things went between Jonas and me earlier in the year——' her sister sat forward confidingly, obviously completely mis-understanding Cassandra's silence '—you needn't be; we were never lovers. Worse luck,' she grimaced with feeling. 'I have a feeling Jonas would make a wonder-fully unforgettable lover. Does he?' she pounced interestedly.

Cassandra had been struck dumb by her sister's opening words—even more so to learn that Joy and Jonas had never—— Good God, that must have been a first for Joy; no wonder she had pursued him so in-tensely for those few months until it became obvious to her Jonas just wasn't interested!

And Jonas hadn't so much as touched Cassandra since the evening he had deliberately set out to prove to her that they were more than capable of enjoying a physical relationship together! Not that she had wanted him to touch her, she inwardly protested. Too much, again...? God, she would be lying if she didn't admit she was still shaken by her physical response to him that night. How could she have been aroused by a man she hated? That in itself was frightening...

'Don't bother to answer; I can see he does!' Joy chuckled as she stood up. 'I have to go and get ready for my evening out with Colin anyway. A word of warning, though,' she added with a grimace. 'Make sure Mummy is among the first to hear of the engagement, otherwise she's likely to throw an embarrassing fit!' She hurried from the room to get ready for her date.

That cage door was closed now, Cassandra realised heavily, the bolt just had to be pushed across, and then there would be no escape . . .

'Mummy, what's an engagement?'

Cassandra was shaken out of her frowning reverie by Bethany's innocently put question, her daughter revealing that once again she hadn't been as deaf to the conversation going on around her as everyone had assumed she was! Cassandra quickly tried to remember what else she and Joy had—— Oh, no!

'And why does Uncle Jonas want to give you a rock?' Bethany frowned her consternation with this puzzling fact. 'It's a strange Christmas present!'

Cassandra laughed with the relief that these were the only two things that seemed to puzzle her daughter about her conversation with Joy. It could have been so much worse!

'It is indeed, my darling.' She stood up to hug her daughter. 'It is indeed!'

Thankfully her mother, Cassandra could tell from her behaviour when she joined them a few minutes later, didn't seem to have heard about the possibility of an engagement between Jonas and herself from the same 'reliable source' Joy had; for once her sister seemed to be acting with a little tact rather than stirring up trouble when she saw the perfect opportunity to do so. That probably had something to do with the fact that Jonas was Colin's boss—— Oh, God, she was getting as cynical as Jonas himself! She should just be grateful for the fact that no one else realised quite how dependent on Jonas they all were for their future . . .

Whatever the reasons for Joy's silence, Cassandra was glad of it, the time spent with her mother passing quite smoothly although a lot of that had to do with their preoccupation with Bethany's rising excitement as the time approached for Father Christmas to come. However, her mother couldn't resist getting in a little dig before they left, about why they couldn't have stayed with her over Christmas instead of going home to spend it alone. Cassandra knew it was useless trying to explain to her mother—yet again—that staying here would have reminded her too much of Christmas last year, when Charles and her father had both still been alive to enjoy it with them . . .

And Cassandra could have done without finding Jonas waiting for them at the house when they arrived home a short time later!

His car was parked in the driveway beside the space where he knew she usually parked her Mercedes, so he had known she wasn't at home before he even got out of his car. But he had gone ahead and rung the doorbell anyway, she realised irritably. And Jean, after his visits all week, wouldn't think twice about letting him wait inside for her to return.

In fact, as she let herself and Bethany into the house with her key, she could hear the murmur of voices coming from the sitting-room, and realised Jean must be in there talking to Jonas still. For some reason Jonas seemed to prefer that small sitting-room where she worked and spent time with Bethany. Although perhaps that wasn't so inexplicable; he seemed intent on invading every private as well as public part of her life!

'Uncle Jonas!' Bethany launched herself across the room at him.

Cassandra entered a little more cautiously, seeing from the laden tray on the table, the steam coming from the teapot spout that Jean had just brought the tray through from the kitchen; Jonas hadn't been here very long, after all.

'I'll go and get a second cup and Bethany's milk,' Jean greeted her with a smile, ruffling Bethany's dark locks affectionately before she went.

Cassandra had fed Bethany her tea before they went to her mother's to deliver the presents, knowing that by the time they got back her daughter would be too excited to even think of eating. She eyed Jonas warily now, unsure, after her conversation with Joy earlier, what his exact purpose was in coming here tonight. He returned her gaze with a rise of mockingly questioning brows.

'Here we are.' Jean bustled back into the room with the extra cup and glass of milk, obviously having had everything prepared in the kitchen.

Cassandra smiled at her gratefully, just about to speak when Bethany chirped up again—and left her standing with her mouth open, gulping in air!

'Uncle Jonas, why are you giving Mummy a rock for Christmas?'

Her intrepid daughter had done it again, frowning up at Jonas now as she sat comfortably ensconced on his knee!

'Don't look at me!' Cassandra protested as he did just that, Jean wisely taking this opportunity to excuse herself hastily on the pretext of preparing dinner, giving

Cassandra a questioning look before she quietly closed the door behind her as she left.

She had been wasting her time earlier at her mother's when she had tried to divert Bethany away from this subject, and obviously failed miserably; Bethany had just decided to wait until she saw Jonas again so that she could ask him for the explanation her mother either couldn't—or wouldn't!—give her.

'Bethany has been listening to her aunty Joy,' Cassandra said, as if that explained everything.

And Jonas looked as if perhaps it did!

'I see,' he mused, smiling down at Bethany as she cuddled up against him. 'Well, it isn't the sort of rock you think it is——'

'But——'

'Hey.' He tapped the little girl playfully on her button-nose. 'You're going to ruin Mummy's surprise for Christmas if you carry on like this.'

'Ulp!' Bethany grimaced before clamping her lips together, shooting Jonas an apologetic look, perfectly understanding this reasoning.

As Jonas had known that she would, Cassandra realised irritably. Why hadn't she thought of that...? Because she wasn't thinking very clearly at all at the moment, she acknowledged resentfully.

'I didn't think,' Bethany groaned apologetically. 'It won't be——'

'Why don't you just drink your milk while Mummy and I have a cup of tea, and let me worry about that, hmm?' Jonas encouraged firmly. 'Then we can all have a game of Mousetrap before your bedtime while Jean is cooking our dinner——'

'Bedtime!' Bethany echoed protestingly. 'But I——'

'You could always try to stay awake this year to see if you can catch Father Christmas delivering the presents into your stocking upstairs,' Jonas added temptingly.

Bethany's eyes went huge at the thought. 'Do you think I might?'

Cassandra certainly hoped not! The last thing she wanted was to wait hours for Bethany to fall asleep before she could even begin organising her presents. And she couldn't stand here and witness the closeness that seemed so natural between Bethany and Jonas, feeling claustrophobic, trapped by their rapport. It was almost as if Jonas already lived here, that she and Bethany were his family. And that they could never be, not even if Jonas did succeed in forcing her into this marriage she didn't want!

'I'll go and find the game,' she suggested desperately, needing to get out of the room for a few minutes at least.

Jonas looked up questioningly, easily reading the panic in her gaze, seeming to mock those feelings. Seeming? He knew exactly how desperate she was feeling as even time worked against her!

Cassandra leaned heavily back against the door once she was outside in the hallway. How was she going to be able to stand this? *How*?

'Why don't you just let me give you the shares, Jonas?' she asked him later, much later, when Bethany was at last in bed, although, Cassandra was sure, not asleep; her daughter was taking Jonas at his word and trying to stay awake long enough to catch Father Christmas in the act! 'My father's ten per cent,' she added as Jonas just looked at her with raised brows, perfectly relaxed as he sat in the armchair opposite her, their meal eaten. 'It's what you want, after all.'

The intimacy of their sitting across from each other like this in the comfort of the small sitting-room, the fire enveloping them in a warm glow, was a completely erroneous one: Cassandra was as tense as a bow-string!

'I want to take care of Bethany too,' he rasped. 'And you will be giving me those shares—as a wedding present!'

She stood up agitatedly. 'And I get your silence as mine,' she scorned. 'That doesn't sound like much of an exchange to me!'

Black eyes narrowed ominously, although Jonas remained sprawled in the armchair, perfectly relaxed in black sweater and dark grey trousers. 'You get a damn sight more than that, and you know it!' he rasped.

Continued financial security for all her family. A secure future for Bethany—something she wanted as desperately as he did. Would he relent if she were to tell him exactly what had happened...? No, came her immediate answer; knowing Jonas, he would still twist it around so that she came out as the villian of the piece. Because he wanted to think that of her. She didn't know quite why; it was just an inescapable fact.

He looked at her with cold eyes. 'I want your answer, damn it,' he grated. 'Now! I've waited long enough.'

She returned his gaze like a cornered rabbit. Good God, she wasn't the hunter, he was, and he was merciless in tracking down his prey!

She frowned. 'Why would you want to marry a woman who doesn't love you——?'

'Love!' he echoed scornfully, sitting forward now. 'I imagined myself in love once.' His mouth twisted self-derisively. 'I quickly learnt that it's a fleeting emotion at best. A trick of the senses——'

'But you're wrong!' She shook her head. 'So wrong. Love is everything.' She held her arms up expressively. 'Being in love with someone is everything. It can make the world a brighter, fuller, happier place——'

'Or a darker, more painful, achingly desolate place!' Jonas put in harshly, a nerve pulsing in his cheek now. 'I don't want love, Cassandra; in fact I would run a mile from it! What I want is your answer,' he repeated uncompromisingly. 'What is it to be, Cassandra, scandal or marriage? The choice is all yours.'

And what a choice it was!

She turned away from the hard cruelty of his face, staring out of the window at the moon as it shone down from the clear starlit sky. A full moon. A hunter's moon...?

God, she was becoming hysterical now. Jonas was only a man—a coldly autocratic man, to be sure, but only a man none the less. And he could be gentle and caring with Bethany, so that core of hardness didn't go all the way though—— Who was she trying to kid? The man was probably kind to children and small animals and merciless to everything else—especially a wife he despised!

But the hunter's moon shone down inexorably—and she heard the lock turn on the cage door...

Cassandra turned slowly back to face him, satisfaction flaring in those probing black eyes as Jonas easily read the resignation on her face. But if he thought he was going to have it all his own way he was mistaken!

'Yes, I'll marry you, Jonas,' she told him flatly. 'But that's all I'll do,' she added even as the light of triumph deepened in his eyes.

A wariness entered his face now. 'What's that supposed to mean?'

Her head went back in challenge, and she sincerely hoped he couldn't see how her legs were trembling with the effort it was taking to stand up to this man who was still such an enigma to her. 'Marriage in name only, Jonas,' she told him shakily. 'That's what I mean.'

He returned her gaze steadily. 'A marriage of convenience,' he finally scorned.

'There's nothing in the least convenient to me about this marriage!' she glared, eyes glowing emotionally.

His very stillness was what was unnerving now. 'Do you really think you're in a position to make conditions?' he spoke softly.

God, how she would love to wipe that satisfaction off his face, knock his legs from under him, tell him to go ahead and do his worst! But she knew that she couldn't do that...

'I can't believe, Jonas,' she told him pityingly, shaking her head disgustedly, 'that you've reached thirty-five years of age without learning that things aren't always what they seem.' She spoke with controlled vehemence now.

His eyes narrowed suspiciously. 'Would you care to explain that remark?'

If he were any other way than he was... 'No,' she said dully, swallowing hard.

'I thought not!' His mouth twisted disparagingly. 'And in this "marriage of convenience", Cassandra, who does get to share your bed?'

'No one.' She shuddered at the thought. 'I don't want that sort of relationship with anyone.'

'Your response to me on Sunday didn't indicate that,' he drawled, brows raised mockingly.

Colour burnt in her cheeks as she remembered all too clearly that time she had spent in his arms; she was still more than a little stunned at her unexpected response to him. She should have known he wouldn't be above reminding her of her weakness; as he had already said himself, he was certainly no gentleman, in or out of business!

'Another one of those occasions, Jonas, when things aren't always what they seem!' she snapped her resentment of his mockery.

'And what about my bed, Cassandra?' he taunted softly. 'Who gets to share that?'

'Whoever you damn well please!' she bit out tautly; this man might scorn love as an emotion but she didn't doubt his sexuality, knew only too well how experienced his lovemaking was, what pleasure a woman could find from his caresses. Which was why she was terrified of sharing his bed herself; if this man made love to her completely, she might forget her dislike of him, and if she did that... It didn't bear thinking about! 'As long as it isn't me, I don't care!' she added vehemently.

Jonas gave her a considering look. 'You aren't going to object if I find myself a mistress?'

She was going to mind being made to look a fool when her brand-new husband took another woman into his life, but the alternative was even more unthinkable! 'I have no guarantee you wouldn't do that anyway, even if we were sharing a bed.' She shrugged dismissively.

'I don't cheat in my relationships!' he rasped coldly, eyes glittering darkly.

'It wouldn't be called cheating if I knew about it, agreed to it,' she encouraged desperately.

Jonas watched her with narrowed eyes as he slowly stood up to cross the room towards her, laughing softly as she took an involuntary step backwards. 'You seem very anxious we shouldn't have a physical relationship, Cassandra,' he taunted softly. 'Why is that?'

Her eyes were wide as he stood directly in front of her now. 'Isn't it obvious?' She at least tried to make an effort to stand up to him, although his proximity was very unnerving. 'A physical relationship between us would make a mockery of everything I believe that sort of closeness should mean between a man and a woman!' But she knew her voice lacked the necessary conviction, Jonas standing only inches away from her now, his nearness working that same mesmerising effect she had known at the weekend when he had taken her in his arms——

As he was now! Strong, enfolding arms that held her against the lean length of his body even as his mouth lowered to claim hers. And as her lips parted moistly beneath his Cassandra knew that she had only been fooling herself the last time he held her like this—that it hadn't been illusion at all, that same aching languor entering her limbs as he began to kiss her with hard demand. She wanted this man—this man who was to be her husband!

She wrenched away from him at this realisation, looking up into that hard, merciless face with wide, bewildered eyes. She had married Charles because she loved him, and their physical relationship had been good even once the initial rosy glow had gone and she had realised Charles wasn't quite as reliable as she might have wished. She didn't love Jonas, and yet she wanted him in a way that shocked and distressed her.

'May the mockery continue,' Jonas told her huskily, eyes black as coal.

Cassandra moved away from him completely. 'I mean it, Jonas,' she told him tautly, hands clenched together in front of her. 'If you insist on going through with this marriage, then it will be in name only.' She was willing to do a lot to protect the people she loved, but sacrificing herself body and soul to this man was something she just couldn't do!

He looked at her consideringly, searchingly, slowly nodding at what he read in her face. 'If you should change your mind...'

'I won't,' she said quickly. Too quickly? Oh, damn the man! 'But I would like an undertaking from you that eventually all your shares will pass on to Bethany.' She met his gaze with unwavering challenge.

Jonas's mouth quirked derisively. 'And I repeat, do you really think you're in a position to make conditions?' he drawled.

Her eyes flashed deeply golden. 'Those shares are Bethany's by right,' she bit out sharply. 'She——'

'Calm down, Cassandra,' Jonas cut in mockingly. 'I'm doing this to protect Bethany's interests, not take anything away from her. I'm wealthy enough in my own right to make provision for any children we might have together——'

'I've just told you,' she flared, her cheeks hot and flushed with the frustration of feeling that this man wasn't even listening to her! 'We won't be having that sort of relationship, so we won't be having any children either!' God, she felt flustered just at the thought of bearing this man's child!

What sort of father would he make? He was very good with Bethany, obviously had no difficulty relaxing with children, and—— They wouldn't be having any children between them! She was relieved that he would probably make a loving stepfather for Bethany, but that would be it!

'If you say so,' Jonas drawled dismissively, obviously bored by the whole subject now.

Bored! Good God, Cassandra's nerves were still shredded by the response she had to this man, and he had lost interest in the subject as if it were only a trivial matter anyway, one that really didn't merit the attention it had already been given!

'Do you think now might be a good time to give you that rock Bethany mentioned earlier?' He crossed the room to the jacket he had draped over the back of the chair, searching through the pockets.

Cassandra tensed at the mere idea of wearing this man's engagement ring. She still wore the rings that Charles had given her so lovingly; how could she now wear Jonas's ring in their place? It would surely weigh on her finger like an iron shackle!

The name discreetly printed on the top of the tiny box was enough to warn her of the exquisite originality of the ring within, but, even so, nothing could have quite prepared her for the dazzling flash of emerald and diamonds when Jonas raised the lid of the box for her to see inside. And yet there was nothing ostentatious about the ring itself; it was just that the heart-shaped emerald in the centre was surrounded by such exquisitely perfect diamonds that they reflected the light in glittering facets. It was a beautiful ring, a ring that should have been bought, and worn, with love.

Cassandra stared at it as if mesmerised, shaking her head. 'I can't wear that,' she told him gruffly, unable to actually look at his face, tears stinging her eyes at the mockery of this engagement.

'If you don't like this ring we can always choose another one——'

'It isn't that,' she protested emotionally, still blinking back the tears.

'Then what is it?' The frown could be heard in his voice. 'Cassandra...?' He raised a hand to lift her chin, frowning as he looked into her face and saw her eyes swimming with tears. 'Cassandra, what——?'

'Mummy...?' A disgruntled voice broke the tension that had suddenly fallen over the room, and both Cassandra and Jonas turned to look at Bethany as she stood so forlornly in the doorway, the rabbit she always took to bed with her rucked under her arm now. 'Mummy, I can't sleep,' she added fretfully. 'And Father

Christmas won't come at all if I don't go to sleep soon!'
she wailed.

Cassandra blinked back the tears, giving her daughter
a watery smile as she crossed to her side. 'Of course he
will, darling.' She went down on her haunches beside
Bethany, smoothing back the ruffled dark hair from the
flushed petulance of Bethany's sleepy face.

'He hasn't put anything in my stocking yet, and——
He hasn't been down here yet either!' the little girl cried
as she saw that the mince-pie, sherry and carrots they
had put out earlier were still untouched on the fireplace.

Cassandra thanked God that they were; they would
have had some serious explaining to do if they had
already disposed of the offerings and yet no presents
had obviously been left yet!

'I haven't gone upstairs to bed yet, darling,' Cassandra
told her daughter soothingly, shooting Jonas a warning
frown when his brows were raised mockingly. She turned
sharply away from that tauntingly speculative gaze; if
things had turned out differently earlier, he was silently
telling her, the two of them might have been in her bed
for Bethany to come and find! 'Everyone has to be asleep
before Father Christmas comes, darling.' She firmly
turned her attention back to her daughter.

Bethany looked slightly less petulant. 'Does that mean
Uncle Jonas is staying with us tonight after all?' she
asked hopefully.

Cassandra deliberately didn't look at Jonas this time;
obviously, as far as Bethany was concerned, she wouldn't
have minded in the least if she had gone to her mother's
bedroom and found not just Cassandra there but
Jonas too!

'Not this time, love,' Jonas answered gently as he moved to join them, bending down to scoop Bethany up easily in his arms.

Bethany frowned down at the open ring-box he still held in one of his hands. 'What's that?'

Cassandra drew in a sharp breath. She had barely had time to accept herself that her marriage to Jonas was going to take place, let alone thought of how she was going to explain it all to Bethany—although she had a feeling, from her daughter's attitude just now to Jonas's staying here, that the child wasn't going to mind too much! And Cassandra could see, from the determination in Jonas's expression, that the matter was going to be taken out of hands anyway, that he intended telling Bethany of the engagement right now! And once Bethany realised what that 'rock' represented, fully understood what an engagement involved, Cassandra had a feeling there would be no turning back, for any of them. There could be no doubt that Bethany adored Jonas, that she was already halfway to accepting him as the paternal figure in her life.

Good God, why didn't she just stop this now? Appeal to Jonas's better nature, tell him the truth—that it hadn't been her father who transferred company funds at all, but Charles . . . !

Because she wasn't sure Jonas had a better nature!

What also kept her silent was that she wasn't sure if knowing Charles had been the one at fault would make any difference to Jonas's demand that she marry him and give him her shares, or if she would be betraying Charles for nothing, Jonas just wanting those shares at any price.

And if, as she thought, Jonas did just want those shares, she wasn't sure how he would react to knowing it was Charles who had taken Hunter and Kyle funds and transferred them into a company of his own...!

Usually her father and Charles had made decisions together concerning which deals they should go for and what they should leave alone, and from the success of Hunter and Kyle that system had worked well enough for the years of their partnership. And then three years ago a property deal had been put to them that Cassandra's father had wanted to stay away from and which Charles had thought they should go ahead with, believing it to be a good investment. He had been so sure it would that he had put his own money in it to start with, along with a loan from the bank. Over the next eighteen months the bottom had dropped out of the property market, as Cassandra's father had predicted that it would, and the bank had called in the loan on Charles's deal. The only way Charles could pay them back was to borrow money from Hunter and Kyle funds, money that should, at least, have been approved by both shareholders. It wasn't, because, as Charles had admitted to her, he had felt foolish after her father had been so certain from the beginning that it wasn't a deal they should have anything to do with! Charles had lost millions, the property he had bought so confidently worth only a quarter of the price he had paid for it.

Charles had told her everything after her father died so suddenly, needing her support, at least. And, of course, he had got it; she was still his wife, no matter how much she might have deplored what he had done

As she was still standing by him, still supporting him, paying the consequences she knew had to be paid...

What would Jonas do with information like that about Charles? The truth of the matter was, she dared not tell him it had been Charles, didn't believe it would make the slightest difference to him if he learnt it had been a member of his own family—a family he despised!—who had committed the fraudulent act, rather than her father as he believed it to be. He had made it perfectly clear that the only reason he wanted to marry her was to safeguard Bethany's future and to secure Cassandra's shares for himself.

Consequently she dared not take the risk of telling Jonas the truth now, knew she would probably be the loser either way, that the outcome would probably be the same no matter what she did, and that Jonas would probably just use that information about Charles to taunt her even more...! It was all those probabilities that actually kept her silent—when she really wanted to scream and shout in protest at her fate!

'This——' Jonas slowly held up the ring-box so that Bethany could look inside '—is the rock I'm giving Mummy for Christmas.' He looked challengingly at Cassandra as he made the announcement.

Bethany giggled as she saw the ring inside the box. 'That isn't a rock, it's a——'

'It's far too late to be getting into a conversation about rocks or rings,' Cassandra cut in sharply, much more sharply than she intended, she realised as Bethany looked across at her with puzzled eyes. 'It really is time you went back to bed, young lady,' she told her daughter determinedly, taking her from Jonas and smiling at her

affectionately to take away any sting there might have
appeared in her voice; she was so tense she was surprised
she wasn't actually shrieking at the top of her lungs the
way a fishwife was reputed to do. No doubt Jonas would
like that! 'If we don't all soon get to bed and go to sleep
Father Christmas may just decide to give us a miss
altogether this year!' she added teasingly, turning as she
reached the doorway. 'Could you just slip the lock on
the front door on your way out, Jonas?' It was her turn
to challenge him now, golden-brown eyes unflinchingly
meeting the dark mockery in his.

'I could,' he drawled mockingly—telling Cassandra
without words that he had no intention of doing so,
though, that he would still be here waiting for his answer
when she came back downstairs.

Bethany was much easier to settle down this second
time; she was actually tired out from the excitement of
the day, her protests only minimal as Cassandra tucked
the duvet round her and kissed her gently on the brow.

'Are you going to bed too now, Mummy?' she
prompted hopefully.

Cassandra only wished that she could—that she could
go to sleep and all of this would have been some awful
nightmare she could wake up from!

'Soon, darling,' she promised. 'I just have to go and
put the lights off downstairs,' and slip the lock on Jonas's
way out!

But she didn't go downstairs straight away; she moved
silently along the hallway to her own bedroom, sitting
down on the bed to look down at the rings she still wore
so proudly on her left hand, the diamond solitaire
Charles had given her on the day he'd asked her to marry

him, the plain gold band he had slipped on her finger on their wedding day three months later. How could she possibly take them off and put that diamond and emerald ring of Jonas's in their place?

Could she tell Jonas the truth? Would he believe her? Would he care?

For all that Charles could be selfish and thoughtless at times, Cassandra had had trouble believing he had done such a thing when he had come to her shortly after her father's death and told her how deeply into debt he had gone. It hadn't seemed possible, seemed incredible to her that Charles could have done such a thing without telling anyone. But she had stood by him anyway; he was her husband, Bethany's father. And she never wanted Bethany to realise that the happy-go-lucky father she had loved so much had actually been so completely irresponsible that he had got them into this mess!

The tears burnt hotly down Cassandra's cheeks as she took off first her engagement ring and then her wedding-ring, transferring them to her right hand, her decision made...

CHAPTER SIX

PETER HUNTER looked frailer than ever on this crisp and clear Christmas morning, sitting in the conservatory having his mid-morning cup of coffee when they arrived, the sun shining brightly through the glass making it feel warmer than it actually was outside.

At seventy-eight Peter's once dark hair was now silver-grey, but he was still a tall, imposing man when he stood up, reed-thin, his gaunt face lined with a lifetime of memories, some happy, many sad. Cassandra had always liked her father-in-law, but felt rather in awe of him at the same time, treating him with the same deference she might a revered grandfather.

Jonas didn't seem to be hampered by the same respectful reserve, not waiting to be invited to sit down in one of the wicker chairs but dropping down into the one nearest his father—possibly because he believed he might be standing a long time if he waited for the invitation to sit down!

'Sit down, Cassandra,' he suggested lightly as she still hovered in the background. 'Don't worry about Bethany; she's perfectly happy in the sitting-room playing with the doll's house you gave her for—Father Christmas gave her for Christmas,' he corrected drily.

Bethany had been overjoyed with the gifts left under the tree for her this morning—and Cassandra had been amazed at the ones left there for her! There had been at least a dozen beautifully wrapped presents that hadn't been there when Cassandra finally went to bed the night before after placing Bethany's gifts there.

Not that her daughter had seemed in the least surprised by the gifts for Cassandra; after all, it was perfectly normal for Father Christmas to leave lots of presents for her mother too, so why should this year be any different?

And as she'd looked at the gaily wrapped presents Cassandra had known exactly who they were from and why they were there. How had been another matter, but that was easily settled after she had spoken quietly to Jean in the kitchen; Jonas had left the gifts for Cassandra with her, to be put under the tree once everyone else was in bed for the night. It wasn't difficult to guess why he had done it, not when she thought of the way Bethany had assured Jonas that her mummy always got 'lots and lots of presents' every year at Christmas; Cassandra certainly didn't fool herself that Jonas had actually bought the lovely gifts to give her pleasure!

Although the fact that he had gone to all that trouble did make the decision she had made the night before seem not quite so horrendous; if Jonas could do something like that for Bethany's sake, then perhaps there was hope for him yet!

As she had known he would be, Jonas had been waiting for her when she got downstairs the night before, and she had duly accepted his proposal and his ring—although since accepting it she had kept the hand wearing that emerald and diamond ring as much out of view as possible——

A fact Jonas seemed more than aware of as she sat down in the chair on the other side of Peter, a dark frown as Jonas's face as she held Peter's gift with her right hand, her left one neatly folded in her lap.

'Happy Christmas, Peter.' She leant forward to kiss her father-in-law on the cheek, handing him the wrapped bottle of malt whisky she knew was his favourite—he always enjoyed a glass of it after his dinner each evening. 'Thank you for the gifts you gave Bethany and me.' She gave a rueful smile at her daughter's absence; after kissing her grandfather hello she had disappeared back into the house to where Jonas had carried her doll's house.

As soon as Bethany had seen the Victorian doll's house, completely fitted out with authentic furniture, her other gifts had unfortunately faded into insignificance. It would have been impossible for them to come out today without bringing the treasured new gift. Although perhaps it was just as well that Bethany was so preoccupied; that challenging glint in Jonas's eyes didn't augur well for this visit!

'Yes, Father,' he drawled now. 'Thank you for what you gave me too.'

Peter's gaze narrowed as he looked at his younger, more enigmatic son. 'I didn't give you anything,' he snapped irritably.

'Exactly,' Jonas derided. 'I'm thanking you for not being hypocritical enough to pretend a Christmas spirit towards me you don't feel!'

Cassandra tensed at the exchange, staring in dismay at the two men, although from their own tense ex-

pressions as they looked at each other she didn't think
either was aware of her presence there at the moment.

Jonas had called for them this morning so that they
could all visit his father together before going on to her
mother's for lunch, although she hadn't intended to visit
her father-in-law until Boxing Day; Cassandra could only
wish now—now that it was too late to avoid this confrontation—that he hadn't! It was the first time she had
seen father and son together, and she wished it could be
the last; the two men obviously couldn't stand each
other! So much for Jonas's excuse that day about not
leaving his father alone all over Christmas; she doubted,
from their behaviour towards each other now, that father
and son had spent more than a few minutes in each
other's company the whole of the last nine months—or
that they had any particular wish to spend much more
time together either!

Peter gave his son a withering look before turning to
Cassandra. 'I hope it's just coincidental that the two of
you arrived here together today...?' He frowned.

'Do you?' Jonas was the one to answer him tauntingly. 'I'm sorry to disappoint you, Father,' he said
without any apology. 'But it isn't!'

Peter ignored him, still looking at Cassandra, eyes the
same blue as Charles's frowningly searching the paleness
of her face. 'Cassandra...?' he finally prompted warily.

She moistened dry lips. God, telling people, people
she cared for, about herself and Jonas was going
to be worse than she had imagined it would be.
'Peter, I——'

'Cassandra and I are going to be married, Father,' Jonas cut in challengingly, obviously feeling none of Cassandra's hesitation.

And why should he? He obviously didn't give a damn what anyone thought of him, or his actions! And Peter looked as if someone had physically struck him, his face grey now, gaunter than ever, his narrowed gaze suddenly seeming almost as dark as Jonas's own as it was turned fiercely on his son. 'Why?' he demanded to know harshly.

Jonas laughed softly, still sitting back in his chair, seemingly relaxed, although Cassandra noticed that his hands tightly gripped the wicker arms beneath them, whether consciously or unconsciously. 'Because we want to, of course,' he drawled dismissively, his gaze unblinking as he unflinchingly returned his father's probing gaze.

Peter looked at his son wordlessly for several minutes—several long, agonisingly tense minutes for Cassandra! Finally he turned to look at her, blue eyes pained. 'Do you want to marry Jonas?' he prompted warily.

She glanced quickly at Jonas, warned by the dark chill of his eyes to be careful what she answered; whatever the arrangement was between them, he didn't want his father to know of it. But she was no more anxious for Peter to know the truth either; exasperated as he too had felt at times by Charles's behaviour, it would probably kill him if he knew just how badly he had behaved this time!

'Of course,' she assured Peter lightly—but it took all her effort of will to withstand the probing look he gave her afterwards, obviously doubting her claim.

Being in the same room with these two men was like being caught in the middle of a storm, waves of resentment flowing between them. After the easy friendship that had existed between Peter and Charles, this contest of wills was nerve-racking!

'Then I repeat, Jonas——' Peter looked at the younger man glacially '—why do you want to marry Cassandra?'

Jonas's mouth quirked. 'I'm not sure that question is exactly complimentary to Cassandra, Father,' he taunted. 'She's a beautiful woman——'

'She's your brother's widow!' Peter cut in harshly.

Cassandra drew in a sharp breath at his vehemence—and at the way Jonas's face had gone white when she dared a glance at him. She might almost not have been in the room now for all the notice he took of her, his icy cold fury directed at his father as he sat forward in his chair, all pretence of being relaxed gone now. 'I know what she is, Father,' Jonas rasped coldly. 'I also know she's going to be my wife.' There was challenge in every taut muscle of his body.

'Don't do this, Jonas,' Peter warned gruffly, pain in his eyes now. 'Leave the past where it belongs—in the past.'

Jonas gave a harshly humourless laugh. 'You can say that to me?' he scorned. 'I've been made to pay for my mother's supposed sins all of my life, and you dare to tell me to leave the past alone!' He shook his head in hard derision, standing up. 'It's time we were leaving, Cassandra,' he told her with icy implacability.

Cassandra had, by this time, believed both men to have forgotten she was there with them at all. In fact, she wished they might have done so for a while longer; their conversation had been revealing, but not revealing enough! What had happened in the past? She knew Peter had divorced Jonas's mother while Jonas was still a young child, that the young boy had remained with his father and older brother after that divorce, but she didn't know the reason for it, or why there was still such resentment between Jonas and Peter after all these years. And she had a feeling she should know—that here was the key to what drove Jonas, why he was as coldly determined as he was.

'Cassandra!' he repeated harshly now, standing tensely beside her chair waiting for her to leave with him.

She stood up abruptly, attempting to smile reassuringly at Peter as he reached out suddenly and clasped her hand, squeezing his hand in understanding for his concern. 'I'll come back and see you before the New Year,' she promised huskily.

'We're getting married then,' Jonas put in hardly.

'So soon?' Alarm flared in Peter's eyes at this news. 'Charles hasn't even been dead a year yet,' he added emotionally.

It was the worst possible thing he could have said; Jonas's mouth tightened ominously at the rebuke. 'Cassandra and I can't wait any longer than the New Year,' he stated firmly, his arm going possessively about her shoulders as he held her to his side, effectively breaking her contact with Peter as he did so. 'Can we?' he prompted her insistently.

She could feel an anger in him, a tense, troubled anger that for once Cassandra felt wasn't directed at her. The last thing Jonas wanted from her, from anyone, she would guess, was sympathy, and yet she knew that at that moment it was exactly what she felt for him.

Whatever had gone wrong between Jonas's mother and Peter, Jonas had grown up with a chip on his shoulder that had followed him even into adulthood. What could have happened twelve years ago to suddenly make him cut himself off from the family completely Cassandra had no idea, but suddenly she knew his life had been a very lonely one, and that a lot of it had been through choice, because he wouldn't allow anyone close enough to hurt him again.

Because of that, he no longer appeared so threatening to her. Which could be very dangerous...

'No,' she answered distractedly. 'We can't wait any longer than that.'

She mustn't think of his gentleness with Bethany, must try only to remember that he was forcing her into this marriage, blackmailing her into it. She couldn't allow her feelings to soften towards this man. She couldn't!

She moved abruptly away from him, disturbed by her own feelings of weakness. 'You'll come to the wedding, Peter?' There was pleading in her eyes as she made the request.

'Mother will be there,' Jonas announced with satisfaction.

Cassandra turned to him sharply. She had assumed, she didn't quite know why, that Jonas's mother must be dead—which was a ridiculous assumption for her to have made, now that she really thought about it; why should

Jonas's mother have died when Peter, ten years his second wife's senior, was still very much alive? Maybe, once again, it was that feeling Jonas gave of being an absolute loner, a man who needed no one and had no one.

But he had a mother... What was she like, this woman Peter had divorced at a time when divorce wasn't quite as commonplace as it was today, a woman who had left her child with his father after that divorce—a woman who had been Charles's stepmother but whom Cassandra had certainly never met as such, and whom Charles and Peter never talked about?

Peter's mouth twisted at the deliberate challenge Jonas had directed at him. 'So will I,' he returned quietly. 'If I'm invited?'

'Of course,' Jonas drawled. 'I wouldn't want you to miss my wedding.'

Peter looked up at him sadly. 'Where did we go wrong with you, Jonas?' He shook his head. 'Where?'

'"We" didn't,' Jonas told him harshly. 'There was only you. And Charles, of course,' he added derisively. 'The Golden Boy.'

Peter flinched at the taunt, although it looked far from the first time he had heard it. 'You're your mother's son, all right,' he rasped disgustedly.

'I'm what you made me,' Jonas scorned. 'Made in your image. You just can't see that.'

His father shook his head. 'Perhaps you are. But you're Claire too, and she——'

'Let's leave my mother out of it!' Jonas bit out harshly. 'After all, you were always so blameless, you and Charles both. You never——'

'Not in front of Cassandra, Jonas.' Peter stood up too now, as tall as his son, but much frailer to look at, the years obviously having robbed him of much more than time; Jonas was the stronger of the two now, both physically and mentally.

'Why shouldn't she hear the truth? She's family!' Jonas hissed in reply, blazing with more emotion now than Cassandra had ever seen in him before. 'And very soon she and Bethany will be my family!' he announced triumphantly.

'The child too...! I had forgotten for a moment.' Peter shook his head wearily, seeming to sway slightly on his feet at the strain this conversation was putting him under. 'Jonas, you can't involve an innocent child like Bethany in this vengeful vendetta you feel towards Charles and me——'

'I was an innocent child,' the younger man reminded him harshly. 'None of you seemed to care about that at the time!'

'But Bethany——'

'Is an adorable child,' Jonas acknowledged coldly. 'I love her already. I could never do anything to harm her. Never,' he grated.

His father looked at him searchingly, at the rigidly set jaw, the nerve that pulsed there, lines etched harshly beside his nose and thinned lips, cold black eyes wide with challenge. And something else... Something far more dangerous.

'Look after them both, Jonas,' Peter finally told him firmly. 'Or you'll have me to answer to!'

Jonas's mouth twisted without humour. 'I'm not a child any more, Father—and I'll do what I damn well please!'

Cassandra knew Jonas spoke the truth when he said he loved Bethany and would never do anything to harm her. But what of Bethany's mother? Cassandra wondered. She had been married to Charles, a man Jonas seemed to think as much responsible for his alienation from his family as his father had been. And she already knew she didn't have that same immunity from Jonas's anger that Bethany had.

But she wanted to know more of the past, had to know exactly what had happened twelve years ago to drive Jonas away. Maybe once she knew that... It couldn't possibly make Jonas despise her any less if she knew, but it just might help her to understand him.

The only worry she had, with a man like Jonas, was that if she understood him she might not hate him any more. And if she didn't hate him she might actually start to love him...

No—she couldn't possibly learn to love a man like Jonas!

'Stay away from my father, Cassandra,' Jonas warned her coldly on the drive to her mother's house, Bethany safely strapped in the back of the car, talking lovingly to the doll Jonas had bought her for Christmas, which seemed capable of doing everything but actually breathing!

Cassandra looked across at him frowningly as she sat beside him in the front of the car. 'He's just a lonely old man, Jonas, and Bethany and I are all he has——'

'He has me too,' he cut in harshly, his hands tightly gripping the steering-wheel now, black eyes staring straight ahead as he drove with controlled speed. 'You've seen how highly he values me!' he scorned bitterly.

She had seen the wealth of pain that existed between the two men, yes. Was it all because of a lifetime's misunderstanding and the fact that Peter had divorced Jonas's mother, or was Charles involved in some way she hadn't even thought of? She did know that nothing she had heard between father and son today had encouraged her to tell Jonas that Charles had been the one to take that money from Hunter and Kyle. She also knew she had to learn the truth, for her own peace of mind as much as anything else.

'Your relationship with your father is nothing to do with me,' she told Jonas now. 'He's still Bethany's grandfather, and I——'

'—intend seeing him when and if you feel like it,' Jonas finished with derision. 'Foolish woman, haven't you realised yet that I don't like being disobeyed?' he mused confidently.

It was that arrogant confidence that infuriated her the most, her eyes flashing deeply gold. 'Foolish man, haven't you learnt yet that I won't be dictated to?' she returned angrily.

'Really?' he returned tauntingly. 'It's my experience that given the right incentive you——'

'Coercion, you mean,' she accused heatedly, her voice kept necessarily low because of Bethany seated in the back of the car—otherwise she would have been shouting once again!

Jonas shrugged unconcernedly. 'Whatever, you respond to it,' he scorned.

And she had thought herself in danger of coming to like this man earlier, of feeling sorry for him, of understanding him. Good God, she understood him all right: he was an arrogant, insufferable, unfeeling swine! She didn't need to know anything else about him.

'I won't be told who I can or can't see, Jonas,' she told him firmly. 'Peter *is* Bethany's grandfather——'

'So you've said,' he rasped. 'And I want you to stay away from him until after our wedding; is that too much to ask?' he said with sarcasm.

In the circumstances, yes! She had told Peter she would go and see him, and go and see him she would. 'Talking of the wedding...' She turned to give a pointed look in Bethany's direction. 'If we're going to tell my mother and Joy about it today then I think we should tell Bethany before we get there.'

Jonas's expression darkened. 'But I thought you had already—— Damn it!' he swore as he manoeuvred the car to the side of the road, stopping the engine to turn and glare at Cassandra. 'I assumed you had told her and she wasn't thrilled with the idea, which was why she hadn't said anything to me about it!' He scowled darkly, glancing in the back of the car at the still engrossed Bethany.

She hadn't told Bethany of her marriage to Jonas because she dreaded her daughter's reaction to the news, but not because she thought Bethany would hate the idea—on the contrary. And, as she had known last night, once Bethany was told there would be no turning back.

She looked at Jonas unflinchingly. 'Why should you have assumed I had told her any such thing? It may have escaped your notice, but I'm not exactly thrilled at the idea of marrying you myself,' she added scornfully.

His mouth twisted. 'Oh, I've noticed. But your aversion doesn't seem to have stopped you accepting—and wearing—my gifts!' He looked pointedly at the silver Celtic-design brooch she had pinned at the throat of the high-necked black sweater she wore.

She knew without looking at it again that it was a beautiful brooch, made out of heavy silver, the black of her jumper a perfect foil for its large intricate design. Cassandra had liked it on sight; in fact she had liked all the things Jonas had had Jean place under the tree for her: the perfume and matching talcum powder, the Swiss chocolates, the beautiful purple wrap-around scarf, the book on Dickens that had both surprised and delighted her; she hadn't realised Jonas had scanned her bookshelves so closely that he had realised the classic writer was one of her favourites. There had also been hand-embroidered hankerchiefs, a lovely figurine in delicate porcelain of a Victorian lady dressed up to go ice-skating, a Domingo CD she hadn't yet bought—one of the few, the opera singer being one of her favourites—something else Jonas seemed to have taken the trouble to find out.

In fact, all of his gifts had been thoughtfully chosen, and coming from anyone else Cassandra would have been thrilled at the care that had been taken selecting them. But this intimate knowledge from Jonas of her likes and dislikes just made her feel more vulnerable and exposed than ever, as if he weren't just taking over her choices in life but all of the things she enjoyed too! She hadn't even thanked him for the gifts yet, had felt too inhibited, as if admitting they were things that gave her pleasure somehow added to their intimacy.

All those lively gifts made the impersonal gold cufflinks she had purchased for Bethany to give to him seem pretty poor in comparison! Although Jonas had assured Bethany he was delighted with them, the two of them laughing together as Bethany helped him put them on.

But Cassandra couldn't help wondering now, after seeing just how estranged things were between Jonas and Peter, just how many other Christmas gifts Jonas had received. If any. He was so much a loner here, and any friends he might have were obviously in America——— Which advanced Cassandra to questioning whether or not there was a particular womanfriend there... He hadn't brought a woman with him when he came back to England nine months ago, but that didn't mean there wasn't someone, that another woman wasn't the reason he had gone back to America so suddenly last week.

But Cassandra had told him she didn't care who shared his bed before or after they were married, and, knowing Jonas, he would take her at her word! Strange how curious she suddenly felt about that faceless shadow of a woman who was probably Jonas's mistress...

Her cheeks felt hot as she realised Jonas was still watching her disparagingly, one of her hands moving self-consciously to the brooch pinned at her throat. 'I thought Father Christmas delivered them?' She looked at him challengingly.

'*Touché*.' He gave an acknowledging inclination of his head before turning fully in his seat to look in the back of the car. 'Bethany?' His quietly firm voice easily attracted the little girl's attention from her play, and Bethany looked up at him curiously. 'How would you like it if your mother and I got married and I came to live with you all the time?'

Cassandra gave a choked gasp at the bluntness with which he had put the situation. Left up to her she would have tried to broach the news a little more gently than that. Although, from the ecstatic look on Bethany's face as she sat forward on her seat to beam up at them, that would have been a waste of Cassandra's time—and her concern that the situation be handled as delicately as possible!

'Really?' Bethany's eyes glowed deeply golden. 'You would really come and live with us forever and ever?'

Jonas smiled at her description. 'Forever and ever,' he nodded.

Bethany sat forward even more to throw an arm about each of their necks. 'That would be wonderful!' She hugged them both tightly before sitting back to clap her hands gleefully. 'Father Christmas did bring my other present after all!' she grinned happily.

Cassandra frowned at her beaming daughter. 'What other present?' she asked warily—already knowing she wasn't going to like the answer!

'Why, that Uncle Jonas should come and live with us, of course,' her precocious daughter answered instantly.

Cassandra was stunned; she had had no idea——!

'Of course,' Jonas murmured mockingly at her side.

Cassandra deliberately didn't look at him, knowing she would scream if she had to look at the triumphant expression on his face. 'And just when did you ask Father Christmas for this particular present?' she asked Bethany drily; she had sat and helped Bethany write her letter to Father Christmas earlier in the month, and there had certainly been no mention of Jonas coming to live with them in that—she would most certainly have remembered it!

Her daughter still grinned from ear to ear, having no idea that her mother wasn't as happy as she was with the idea of Jonas coming to live with them forever and ever! 'We had to write a letter to put in the school postbox for Father Christmas, and as I had forgotten to put in my other letter about Uncle Jonas coming to live with us I asked the teacher to help me write it in this one.'

Cassandra couldn't help wondering what Mrs Grayson had made of that!

'Father Christmas has a lot to answer for,' she muttered disgustedly.

'Look on the bright side,' Jonas chuckled at her side. 'She could have asked for something really impossible.'

Until a week ago Cassandra had believed the idea of her marrying Jonas and his coming to live with them forever and ever *was* impossible!

CHAPTER SEVEN

'NEXT week!' Marguerite gasped disbelievingly, having initially been thrilled at the announcement that Cassandra and Jonas were to be married—until she had learnt the speed with which it was to take place!

Jonas had waited until they were all seated around the table for lunch, Joy and Colin, Marguerite and Godfrey—the elderly man had spent Christmas with the family for as long as Cassandra could remember—Bethany, Jonas and Cassandra, before telling the rest of the family they were engaged to be married.

Joy had given Cassandra a smile of knowing mockery, Colin had congratulated them, Godfrey still looked dazed by the whole thing, and Marguerite—well, her first reaction had been something that looked a little like relief, quickly followed by the pleasure—so quickly that Cassandra wondered if she could possibly have imagined that initial response... Because now her mother just looked horrified!

'We can't possibly organise a wedding for next week!' she protested now, shaking her head.

'*We* aren't going to,' Jonas informed her quietly, his hand possessively on Cassandra's as it rested on the table-top. 'Cassandra and I are both adults, perfectly capable of organising our own wedding,' he stated abruptly.

Marguerite frowned at this dismissal of her help. 'But surely I——'

'Besides,' Jonas added firmly, 'it's going to be a very quiet affair. Cassandra and I both want it that way.'

Cassandra would like it kept so quiet that no one actually knew about it!

Her mother shook her head dazedly, lunch completely forgotten. 'It's all very sudd—— There isn't anything I should know about, is there, dear?' She looked worriedly at Cassandra.

Cassandra returned her gaze searchingly, wondering if her mother had begun to understand her at last, that she actually realised—and cared!—that there was something decidedly odd about this sudden marriage to Jonas. But what she read in her mother's anxious expression disgusted her rather than filled her with relief.

'There aren't any little Hunters on the way, Mother, if that's what you're so delicately implying,' she drawled hardly. 'Jonas and I have another reason entirely for marrying so hastily——' She broke off abruptly as Jonas's fingers tightened painfully about hers, biting back the relieved sigh as that grip loosened now that it had had the desired effect of silencing her.

What had he thought she was going to do—blurt out the truth, throw herself on the mercy of her family? She knew better than to even try to do that!

'We're in love, Marguerite,' Jonas drawled. 'We want to be together. I'm sure you know how that feels.'

'Don't make such a fuss, Marguerite.' Godfrey beamed at the 'happy couple'. 'I'm sure you must remember how you and David felt in those early days together.'

Cassandra knew that her parents had had a good marriage, that her mother had been devastated by her husband's death, but she certainly couldn't ever imagine her mother in those first heady days of being in love, when all that seemed to matter was being with the person you loved. Jonas in that role was even more unbelievable!

'Well, of course.' Her mother was still slightly flustered at the speed with which things were happening. 'But even so it does seem——'

'It's what we both want, Marguerite.' Jonas's voice had hardened now, although he remained outwardly relaxed, his hand lightly clasping Cassandra's.

'May as well accept the inevitable with good grace, my dear,' Godfrey told Marguerite affectionately. 'Men like Jonas don't want to be messing about with long engagements, and then yards of lace and orange blossom!'

'I couldn't have put it better myself, Godfrey.' Jonas smiled at the older man, knowing he had found an ally. 'Now I suggest we all eat our lunch before it gets cold.' He looked at them all pointedly, obviously welcoming no more criticism of his plans—or receiving any! Jonas had said they should eat their lunch, and that was just what they all did.

Cassandra wished she could have enjoyed the perfectly cooked Christmas lunch with as much gusto as the others seated at the table seemed to do, the conversation noisy, Bethany allowed to get up and pull everyone's cracker with them, more often than not ending up with the gift that had been inside too. As far as her daughter was concerned, all was right with the world...

Whereas Cassandra wasn't sure her world would ever be right again!

'Well, I think everyone took the news very well, don't you?' Jonas said with satisfaction, the day over, the three of them back at Cassandra's house now, Bethany asleep upstairs, having been carried up there by Jonas after falling asleep in the back of the car on the drive home, the excitement of the day having finally worn her out.

Jean had already returned from her sister's house, where she had spent her usual Christmas day, and gone to bed by the time they got in, and Cassandra had assumed that once Jonas had carried Bethany upstairs he would leave so that she could go to bed too.

But as usual Jonas had his own ideas about how he should behave, and by the time Cassandra had settled Bethany in her bed for the night Jonas had gone downstairs to the sitting-room and lit the fire before making himself comfortable in one of the armchairs beside it, warming a glass of brandy in the lean strength of his hands, then sipping it appreciatively, giving no impression of leaving in the immediate, or even near future.

Cassandra sat down in the chair opposite him, well aware of how cosy and homely they must appear sitting here together—when all the time she felt like crying. In fact, she was going to do just that if Jonas didn't leave soon!

'Yes,' she finally answered him huskily; she hadn't expected any dissenting voices from her family when they were told she was to marry Jonas!

Jonas looked across at her searchingly, black gaze enigmatic as he took in her too pale cheeks and overbright eyes. 'Cassandra?' he prompted softly.

She swallowed hard, fighting back the tears that had been threatening to fall all day. 'It's late, Jonas. It's been a long day, and I—I'm tired.'

He stood up to slowly cross the short distance that separated them, coming down on his haunches beside her to raise her chin with gentle fingers, looking deep into the shadowed depth of her eyes. 'What is it, Cassandra?' he finally asked gruffly.

She gave a choked laugh, her throat full of tears too now. What was it? It was everything! The day. Her family. Jonas. She had spent the day surrounded by the people closest to her—her daughter, her family, the man she was going to marry—and she had never felt so alone and lonely in her whole life!

All of it—the unwrapping of gifts, the family lunch and tea, the congratulations of her family on her forth-coming marriage, Bethany's heady excitement with the day, Jonas's brooding presence at her side—in fact, everyone had behaved today exactly as she had thought they would. So why did she feel so depressed about it?

She shook her head self-derisively. 'I'm just being silly,' she dismissed ruefully, the tears thankfully re-ceding with this realisation.

Jonas's mouth twisted. 'That isn't an emotion I've ever associated with you,' she murmured drily.

Cassandra was very conscious of his hands still resting against her jaw, lightly caressing now, like tiny electric shocks against her skin. 'Oh, believe me, Jonas, I can be silly. Very silly,' she added with heavy emotion. It would pass, she knew it would pass, but until it did...

He gave a puzzled frown at the strangeness of her mood, coming to sit on the arm of her chair, tilting her chin up now so that she looked straight into the brooding darkness of his face. Only it wasn't brooding or dark at this moment; his eyes were gentle with concern, his harsh features softened into a questioning frown as he still looked searchingly into her face.

Cassandra barely had time to blink her surprise at this unexpected emotion before his head began to lower slowly towards hers, every bone in her body seeming to melt completely as his mouth claimed hers in the most piercingly sensual caress she had ever imagined.

For a moment, only a brief stunned moment—to her everlasting shame it was very brief!—Cassandra neither responded nor resisted. And then her lips began to move against his, her arms moving up about his neck as she pulled him down to her, pleasure singing through her veins as she felt truly alive for the first time today.

Jonas slid down the side of the chair, both of them sitting in the well of it now, the whole length of their bodies touching from shoulder to knee. Cassandra felt her breasts crushed against Jonas's chest, but it was a near-pain she welcomed, loving the hard pressure of Jonas's body against hers as their kisses deepened, no longer gently searching but becoming increasingly fevered as passion soared and took over from any other emotion. In fact, no other emotion existed!

She felt heat against her bared flesh as Jonas pushed aside her jumper, but it wasn't the fire that warmed her but the heat of his own body as he pressed even closer to her, disposing of his shirt as if it were an old rag rather than the silk it really was, only the thin wisp of Cassandra's bra separating their bared torsos now.

And still Jonas's mouth played havoc with her senses, drinking deeper and deeper, moist tongue probing, searching, flitting over teeth and tongue before plunging down, down, hands cradling either side of her flushed face as his tongue possessed her in the way his throbbing need told her he wanted to.

Without moving his mouth from hers, Jonas gently pulled her down on to the rug in front of the fire, his arms moving about her body now, those hands caressing the slender length of her back, the gossamer silk that had separated them disappearing as if by magic, Cassandra's breasts tautly free; she gasped low in her throat as one of his hands moved to cup her there, the thumbtip moving lightly over the already hardened nipple, each caress intensifying the burning ache she felt between her thighs.

His lips left hers now to travel the length of her throat, down over the silky flesh to the upward thrust of her other breast, Cassandra watching as if mesmerised as his tongue flicked out to wet that nipple, licking slowly, tantalisingly over the fiery tip as she felt her body arching towards him for more, much more, her hands moving up to cradle the back of his head as he at last drew the nipple fully into the moist cavern of his mouth, alternately sucking and licking the throbbing tip until Cassandra cried out with a deeper need.

His hands caressed now, stroking up and down the length of her spine, coming to rest on the slenderness of her hips, pushing aside the clothing there as if it was of no consequence at all, touching her naked thighs and legs, groaning low in his throat at the feel of her silken flesh beneath his hands.

Cassandra touched him too, hands moving over the firm flesh of his broad shoulders, marvelling at the play of muscles beneath the tanned skin; then her hands moved down his back, feeling a tautness in him that matched her own.

Her movements seemed awkward and clumsy as she tried to rid him of his clothing too, wanting to feel him fully naked against her, desperate to know the feel of that silken hardness of his thighs as they throbbed against her. Their breathing was ragged now as desire was heightened by naked flesh against naked flesh, hands questing, mouths searching.

Jonas's body looked magnificent in the firelight, hard golden flesh, all light and shadow; he was beautiful!

'Touch me!' he groaned as he saw the hunger in her flushed face. 'For God's sake, Cassandra, I need you to touch me!'

As she needed to touch him, needed it so badly that she trembled with the desire, hands and fingertips once again moving caressingly over the hard contours of his body, touching the hard muscles in his back before moving down further to his hips, his buttocks, hesitating in her caresses as he gave a low, strangulated groan at the caress of her silken fingertips on his tautly hard flesh.

'Don't stop!' he groaned now. 'Oh, God, don't stop, Cassandra. I need—I want—— Oh, God!' He shuddered in ecstasy-pain as she gave him what he wanted, the hardness of his thighs leaping almost out of control now. 'I want to give you—you need—I don't think I can wait any longer, Cassandra!' he moaned as he gathered her into his arms and crushed her against him, burying his face in the length of her silken hair as he breathed deeply of its perfume, fighting for control, for the time to give her pleasure as she had given it to him.

But Cassandra didn't want to wait any longer either, wanted the deeper pleasure from him that his caresses promised, a burning pleasure that she ached for, that every particle of her body cried out for. 'Now, Jonas,' she pleaded huskily. 'Please make it now!'

His gaze held hers as he lowered her to lie back on the rug, black eyes burning into gold as the firelight flickered across her body in a golden caress of its own and he slowly lowered himself to her, entering her, slowly, filling her in a way that drove everything else from her thoughts but the feel of Jonas pulsating inside her, moving now, slowly, surely, stroking the flames inside her higher and higher even as his mouth closed over hers, swallowing up her low moans of ecstasy.

Bodies moved together in perfect harmony, flicking tongues matching it, accompanied by low moans of pleasure that neither was aware of making as the crescendo inside them rose to a pitch that couldn't be controlled, skin damp from their heated contact now as they moved moistly together in a rhythm that was as beautiful as any ballet.

Cassandra felt the ache building inside her to an un-stoppable heat that reached every muscle and nerve-ending, down to her fingertips, to the tips of her toes, lids flying wide open as she looked up into the dark beauty of Jonas's face at the moment she felt the fire burst out of control, holding him to her as she felt totally possessed, enveloped, Jonas reaching that same heady plateau with her; she watched him, the taut ecstasy in his face, his throat arched, every muscle straining against her as their pleasure exploded together, tremor after tremor continuing to rack their bodies long after their heady gasps had quietened to low groans of release.

Jonas collapsed weakly against her, his face buried in her perfumed throat, his breathing ragged and deep as he lay against her, their bodies still entwined, one of her hands slowly caressing the damp hair at his nape.

Cassandra was no longer fooled by her unhappiness today, knew it had nothing to do with her father not being there, nothing to do with Charles not being there either. The reason she had been so troubled and unhappy today came from another reason entirely, from something that had been forcing itself into her consciousness since they visited Peter this morning.

Somewhere, somehow—oh, God, she didn't know how!—she had fallen in love with Jonas!

How long had she been running away from that knowledge? Since last night when she had told him she wanted the marriage to exist in name only? Since Jonas had told her he wanted to marry her? Before that?

Oh, God, she didn't know when she had begun to love this man who could be so hard and unyielding with anyone who opposed him, and yet so gentle with a child he knew loved him! Maybe that was when she had begun to love him too. Because she did love him.

Could she have fought him more strongly over his demand that she marry him and give him her shares as a wedding gift, or had she secretly welcomed the excuse to become his wife? Not then, she assured herself heavily; then she had been too busy denying her own feelings for this man to realise what she wanted. But now? Now she wanted to be his wife. Because she loved him—this man who had told her he would run away from any love that was offered to him!

What had confused and deceived her about her feelings towards Jonas was that loving him was nothing like loving Charles had been. Charles, for all that he had been in his forties when they married, had been like a child who needed protecting, from himself as much as anything else. With Jonas it was the opposite: he wanted to protect. And whenever she was with him she felt singingly alive, more alive than she had ever felt in her life before.

Charles . . .

What would he make of this love she had for his younger half-brother? Whatever animosity there had been between the two men in the past, Charles had tried to bridge the gulf by inviting Jonas to their wedding, a gesture that had been clearly rebuffed. But Charles had tried again, by leaving Jonas such a large portion of his shares on his death, something Jonas hadn't rejected, although he clearly didn't need the shares or the headache the company had brought with it—not if his personal wealth was all that he claimed it was, and she had no reason to doubt it. Had Charles realised Jonas was probably the only one who could turn the company around? Even if it was in this way!

And yet she loved Jonas . . .

'What are you thinking about?'

She had been so lost in the terrible wonder of her feelings for this man that she hadn't even realised he was now watching her with narrowed dark eyes, the stilling of her caressing hand against his nape seeming to have been what alerted him to her preoccupied thoughts.

Cassandra looked up at him with pained eyes, longing for the return of the passionate lover she had known only minutes ago, the man who had wanted only to give to her.

But already the coldly wary Jonas was taking that man's place, his expression grim as he moved to lie at her side. 'You're thinking of him, aren't you?' he accused harshly, moving to pull on his clothes with unhurried force.

The blaze of colour that instantly heightened her cheeks gave her away, and she gave a choked cry of protest as Jonas stood up forcefully, disgust etched in every hard line of his face as he looked down at her.

'It wasn't like that, Jonas,' she told him beseechingly, sitting up.

For a moment, a very brief moment, he seemed transfixed by her naked beauty in the golden firelight, and then the coldness returned to his expression. He turned away, fully dressed now, dragging his jacket from the back of the chair where he had thrown it earlier. 'You can have your "marriage of convenience", Cassandra,' he rasped viciously. 'I have no intention of taking Charles's place in your sensual imaginings ever again!'

'But it——'

'Don't bother to get up,' he scorned her lack of clothing as he looked down at her contemptuously. Cassandra instantly felt self-conscious in her nakedness in the face of such angry derision, reaching out to clutch her sweater to her now, a fact Jonas viewed with a scornful twist of his mouth. 'I can see myself out!'

'Jonas, please!' she managed to cry out as he reached the door. 'Let me explain!'

He turned briefly. 'There's nothing to explain. I hope you enjoy your memories of your dead husband, Cassandra,' he added hardly. 'Because this one will never share your bed again!' He slammed out of the room, and she heard him slam out of the house two seconds later.

She rolled over and buried her face in her hands, crying as she hadn't cried since Charles died. In some ways this pain was even worse than losing Charles had been. And she had years stretching ahead of her as Jonas's wife, years of loving a man who hated and despised her...!

CHAPTER EIGHT

'YOU'RE supposed to look like this after the honey-moon, Cassandra, not before,' Joy taunted softly.

'Hmm?' Cassandra looked at her sister vaguely, lost in her own thoughts.

She had just brought Bethany over to spend the afternoon with her grandmother, having an appointment herself this afternoon that she would rather Bethany—and Bethany's ears, especially!—weren't present at.

Unfortunately, it seemed she had to run the gauntlet of her sister's enigmatic remarks before she could make her escape; Bethany had already set off in search of her grandmother, after having been informed she was in the dining-room arranging flowers.

Joy grinned at her knowingly. 'Dark shadows under the eyes from lack of sleep!' she supplied suggestively.

Cassandra knew her sister was right about the dark shadows, and Joy was also right about them being caused from lack of sleep—but it wasn't for the reason she was implying!

The truth of the matter was Cassandra had found little comfort in sleep since Christmas Day. In fact, she had found little comfort in anything since that day, didn't even know how she had got through the rest of Christmas without actually breaking down!

Jonas seemed to have been at her side every minute of the day, an ominous presence, even the mocking humour gone from him now. He hardly gave the impression of being a newly engaged man! And as such the speed with which he was organising the wedding must hardly seem credible to anyone observing the two of them together; they didn't so much as touch, let alone seem desperate to 'be together'!

But Jonas had organised the wedding—not before the New Year, as he had wanted, but for January the second, which was just as good in his eyes—the first working day after the long festive holidays. The day he would make sure the accounts were correct for the year-end audit...

The only time Jonas pointedly left her alone was at night. And it was during those long sleepless nights that Cassandra thought of him, remembering everything about that single time he had made love to her. If he was to be believed—and she had never found a single reason to doubt he always meant what he said!—then it was a memory that was going to have to last her a lifetime.

Joy had been right: Jonas did make an unforgettable lover—so unforgettable that Cassandra ached for him to make love to her again...!

'Not that I thought for one moment that Jonas would wait for your wedding night,' Joy dismissed drily. 'But I'm a little surprised at you, Cassandra,' she added tauntingly. 'Couldn't resist seeing if I was right, hmm?' She arched dark brows, eagerly inviting confidences.

Considering the two of them had never been close enough for Cassandra to want to confide in her sister in the past, she certainly wasn't going to break the habit of a lifetime where Jonas was concerned. Especially not when Joy was so near the truth!

'Tell Mummy I'll be back as soon as I can,' she told Joy briskly, not willing to get into any sort of conversation about her relationship with Jonas; it was non-existent at the moment, anyway. Jonas couldn't even be bothered to acknowledge her presence most of the time, giving most of his attention to Bethany. Not that her daughter objected, and neither did Cassandra in this instance; it was important that Jonas and Bethany form an emotional bond, and she was feeling too raw herself at the moment to be able to contend with his verbal sparring with any degree of dignity.

'Off to meet Simeon?' her sister taunted, obviously piqued now at not getting the reaction from Cassandra that she wanted over her teasing, knowing very well that she hadn't seen Simeon on a social level since she became engaged to Jonas. 'Or are you and Jonas sneaking off for a romantic afternoon together?' she drawled mockingly, both of them knowing Jonas was hardly the type to 'sneak' off anywhere, let alone for a romantic afternoon.

'I should be back before tea,' Cassandra continued with her own conversation regardless. 'But if I should happen to be delayed...'

'I'm sure we can manage to feed Bethany,' Joy assured her in a disgruntled voice. 'Great inconvenience these school holidays, aren't they?' She frowned.

Cassandra had never thought so, either now or in the past. In fact, she was sure she would have gone insane these last few days without Bethany at home to keep her spirits up. Nothing could seem quite so black and gloomy with her sunny daughter at her side!

'Bye, Joy,' she said drily, moving to the open doorway.

'I'm looking forward to the rehearsal this evening,' her sister called after her softly.

Cassandra stiffened, turning slowly, knowing she must have paled.

'At the church, for the blessing,' Joy added knowingly, blue eyes sparkling mischievously. Only there was nothing in the least amusing or funny to Cassandra about the rehearsal this evening, as she was sure her sister very well knew!

She didn't make any reply, letting her sister have the last word as she seemed so determined to. And what a last word it was!

Because of the speed with which she and Jonas were to be married the actual marriage was to take place in a register office, but Jonas had been insistent that they should have a blessing performed in the local church, and as they were marrying on a weekday this hadn't posed any problem for the vicar to fit into his schedule. To Cassandra, having their marriage, a marriage based on distrust, blessed in church seemed like a mockery of everything the marriage ceremony should truly mean.

'Not that you need the rehearsal,' Joy continued bitchily. 'But I suppose Jonas might. At least...I presume that he does?'

'Goodbye, Joy,' Cassandra told her firmly, making good her escape this time before her sister could drop any more bombshells.

The truth of the matter was it had never occurred to her to question whether or not Jonas had been married before! But she was sure he couldn't have been; didn't he mock the very idea of his ever caring for anyone enough to make such a commitment for love? Although he had also said he had believed himself in love once...

No, she couldn't believe Jonas had ever been married; it was the sort of thing he would have told her—— But would he? Wasn't Jonas a law unto himself?

But Peter would know if his youngest son had ever been married—and it was Peter she was going to see this afternoon. It hadn't been easy, organising this time to go and see her father-in-law, with Jonas constantly at her side these last few days—as if he was well aware of her desire to go and see Peter, despite his instruction that she shouldn't, and he was doing his best to thwart her plans to do so. But after days of being out of the office a meeting had come up today that Jonas just couldn't avoid going to, giving Cassandra an unexpectedly free afternoon; although he hadn't told her about the meeting until lunchtime! But luckily Peter was able to see her at almost any time, and he had seemed more than pleased to hear from her when she telephoned after lunch, once Jonas had left for his meeting, and asked to go and visit him. She hated being made to feel slightly underhand like this, but an out-in-the-open confrontation with Jonas was something she didn't feel strong enough to cope with just now.

As it was, she viewed the following meeting with a mixture of anticipation and fear; she was at last going to hear the truth about the past, and yet at the same time she wasn't sure she wanted to...!

She would tell Jonas she had seen Peter, of course, had no intention of keeping it from him indefinitely;

that just wasn't her way. But she knew there was going to be an argument over it, an argument she might feel better able to deal with after talking to Peter. It was for her own peace of mind that she was going to see him this afternoon; she had to know more about Jonas before she married him than that she loved him! Maybe if she did there would be some hope for them. She had to believe that!

Peter was once again out in the conservatory when she arrived; in fact he seemed to spend a lot of his time out there nowadays, tending his plants, or just gazing out over the grounds of the house—the gardens where Charles and Jonas had once played as children...?

Cassandra stood in the doorway for several minutes watching the elderly man unobserved, having assured the butler she was more than capable of showing herself through. Peter was staring out across the beautifully tended lawns and towering oak trees, a fine dusting of snow on both.

Bethany had been delighted this morning when she got out of bed to look out of the window and had seen the snow there. In fact, she probably had her poor grandmother out playing snowballs in it right now, Cassandra thought ruefully.

Did Peter see another picture other than the white stillness outside, a time when his two sons had played unconcernedly out in the snow too, laughing as they made snowballs and threw them at anything that moved, including each other? Or had Charles and Jonas never had that sort of close relationship? There had been thirteen years' difference in their ages, after all.

Jonas as a child. It was hard to envisage. What had he been like then?

Peter turned at that moment, saw her standing wistfully in the doorway, and got slowly to his feet. 'I hoped you would come,' he said softly.

She gave him a smile of affection. 'I told you that I would.'

'Yes,' he acknowledged gently, taking one of her hands into his. 'But I wasn't sure you would.'

Because of Jonas. He knew his youngest son didn't want her to visit him.

Cassandra squeezed Peter's hand understandingly before releasing it. 'Let's sit down, shall we?' she suggested lightly. 'I'm afraid I didn't bring Bethany today,' she apologised ruefully as they both sat down.

'No,' he accepted without question. 'You want to know about Jonas,' he sighed, his gaze troubled.

She didn't *want* to exactly, but she *needed* to.

Peter was watching her closely now. 'Do you love him?' he finally asked.

She swallowed hard, her gaze unwavering on his. 'Yes.'

'Does he love you?'

'No,' she answered without hesitation; what had happened between them on Christmas Day certainly hadn't been love on Jonas's part.

Peter frowned. 'Then could you possibly tell me why you're marrying him?'

She wasn't sure herself of that any more! Which had come first, her inner knowledge that she loved Jonas in spite of herself, or his demand that she marry him? The latter had certainly taken away any difficult probing into her emotions. Until now. She had lain awake these last few nights trying to find the answers, and she still didn't have any that she felt comfortable with. Which was another one of the reasons she was here today. 'Isn't it enough that I love Jonas?' she answered evasively.

'With Jonas, no,' his father sighed resignedly. 'God knows, Jonas isn't an easy man to love—and I should know!' He shook his head. 'No, that isn't what I meant at all.' Peter seemed to be talking to himself now, almost forgetting that Cassandra was in the room with him. 'Jonas is easy to love; after all, he's my son. But he doesn't accept love, he never has. No, that isn't strictly correct either.' He was becoming impatient with himself at his inability to explain what he meant.

But Cassandra, of all people, knew exactly what he meant; wasn't that the reason she was here, to find out why Jonas rejected love from his life?

'To understand Jonas at all, I think you have to know the family history too,' Peter told her now gruffly. 'I married Kathleen, Charles's mother, when I was twenty-two and she was just eighteen.' His voice had softened, his expression gentle with love as he spoke of his first wife. 'We were young, in love with each other and with life, in no hurry to have children because we were still very much children ourselves. Consequently, by the time we did have Charles, we were both more than ready for the responsibility that comes along with being a parent. He was our golden child——' He broke off as he saw the way Cassandra flinched at the description, his mouth twisting ruefully. '"Golden Boy", Jonas calls him, I know,' he nodded.

And Jonas was the opposite: dark, brooding, unapproachable...

Peter shrugged. 'I accept a lot of the blame for the animosity that existed between my two sons—I spoilt Charles.' He gave a heavy sigh. 'But when Charles was ten Kathleen was killed in a skiing accident. Just one of those inexplicable things, but it robbed me of the woman I loved.' He seemed lost in memories now. 'Made our son that much more precious.'

Cassandra could see how the tragedy still haunted him. But he had married again, had Jonas in that second marriage...

Peter looked up, easily reading her puzzled thoughts, his expression once again rueful. 'I'm sure it seems strange to you that I married again within two years of Kathleen's death, but——'

'It shouldn't,' she accepted self-derisively; wasn't she about to do the same thing?

'I was lonely,' Peter sighed, resting his head back in the chair. 'Claire, Jonas's mother, was someone we had occasionally met at parties, not exactly a friend, but a frequent acquaintance. She was—kind to me after Kathleen died, understanding, always willing to sit and listen, a shoulder for me to cry on, if you like. It's no excuse, but—I married Claire for all the wrong reasons,' he breathed shakily. 'But maybe you could also say she married me knowing I was still grieving for another woman,' he frowned.

Cassandra would say, in the circumstances, he could definitely say that!

'Whatever,' Peter dismissed abruptly, 'we married. She resented Charles, the time I spent with him, the love I had for him, claimed I cared more for him that I did for her. She was right, of course,' he frowned. 'Our marriage was a disaster. But by the time we realised that Claire was already pregnant.'

'Jonas...' Cassandra realised achingly. God, poor Jonas; his parents' marriage was over even before he was born! How long had it taken him to realise that? Or had he always known?

'Yes,' Peter acknowledged heavily as he saw the emotions chasing across her face. 'An innocent child, born into a battlefield. And by the time Jonas was born it had become at least that. Claire's resentment towards Charles grew with the birth of her own child, so much so that she tried to push Charles out completely, to persuade me to make Jonas my sole heir. When I refused to do that she turned Jonas against both Charles and me, told him he wasn't wanted—— God knows what she didn't tell him!' he said harshly. 'She alienated Jonas from us completely, while at the same time living her own separate life from us, having her own friends, mostly male. The marriage was hell. Charles knew what was going on, of course, and he got off to university as soon as he could, hated having to live in a battlefield, so he didn't witness all the fights between Claire and me, both verbal and physical; Claire felt no compunction at all in hitting out at me when things didn't go the way she wanted them to!'

Cassandra couldn't imagine this nobly proud man having to deal with emotions as basic as that, knew how he must have hated it—and also the reason he had stood it for as long as he obviously had. There could have been only one reason: Jonas. His younger son. A son deliberately brought up to distrust him and resent his older brother...!

Peter shook his head with remembered bitterness. 'By the time Jonas was eight I knew I couldn't live like that any more, felt too battered emotionally after one particularly vitriolic outburst, over Claire's latest lover, as I recall, to go on with it any more,' he added disgustedly. 'But I couldn't let Jonas go and live with his mother if there was to be a divorce; I knew she would poison his life completely if I allowed that. And so there was a nasty custody case.' His mouth thinned with the distaste of having to publicly reveal the intimate details of his second marriage. 'At the worst point of the hearing, when Claire could see she was probably going to lose, she told the court I wasn't Jonas's father anyway, so had no right to him...!' He shook his head with a pained wince.

Cassandra stared at him with wide eyes; Jonas wasn't his son...?

'It was a lie, of course,' Peter instantly dismissed the very idea of that being true. 'The last viperous thrust of a rattlesnake! For all her adulterous ways once our relationship was over, I had never at any time doubted that Jonas was my son.' He looked up and saw how pale Cassandra had become, smiling at her without any real humour. 'Remind me to show you a photograph of Jonas's paternal grandfather some time,' he drawled. 'Jonas is him all over again; he was an old curmudgeon too!'

This more than accurate description of Jonas released some of the tension, and Cassandra found herself returning Peter's smile with humour now. 'I would love to see some old photographs of your family. And Jonas,' she added huskily.

Peter leant forward to squeeze her hand understandingly. 'And so you shall. Over a cup of tea. Once we've disposed of all of the past,' he added grimly, sitting back in his chair once again.

She moistened dry lips. 'What happened to make Jonas go to America twelve years ago? And what is the rift between Charles and Jonas?' She looked at him enquiringly.

'As you've probably already guessed,' Peter sighed wearily, 'the two are connected. The rivalry that Jonas felt towards Charles, which Claire had instilled in him from birth, continued even after Claire had left the house. Claire virtually disappeared from his life for years after the divorce, and the easiest way for Jonas to deal with that was to blame Charles and me. And maybe I was to blame.' He shook his head. 'I certainly didn't encourage the relationship, and Claire wasn't one for putting herself out, least of all for a child who couldn't do anything for her in return. I'm sorry,' he winced. 'I must be painting a very bitter picture. But——'

'It's all right, Peter,' Cassandra hastened to reassure him, having so much more insight now into what had made Jonas the man he was—and needing to know the rest!

'He's useful to her again now, of course,' Peter rasped, eyes narrowed angrily. 'Which is why the relationship exists, on some sort of level.'

Jonas had made no effort that Cassandra knew of to see his mother over the Christmas holiday, or to introduce the two women. But she did know he had invited his mother to the wedding in four days' time, as he had said he would...

Peter shook his head. 'But all through those difficult years with Jonas, teenage and adolescent, Claire didn't want to know, except for the odd outing. It was because of that, I'm sure, that the relationship between Charles and Jonas improved slightly. Charles went into business with your father, and Jonas went on to university——' He broke off as Cassandra gasped, looking at her enquiringly.

'It had never occurred to me before that Jonas was still in England when Daddy and Charles formed Hunter and Kyle,' she explained almost dazedly. She couldn't think why she hadn't—her father and Charles had been in partnership for fifteen years before they both died.

It seemed strange to think she could have met Jonas all those years ago, if things hadn't been so strained between him and Charles... Admittedly, she would only have been thirteen years old when Jonas went off to America, but just to have seen him once before whatever rift had driven him to leave in the first place...! Perhaps, in retrospect, he wouldn't have been all that different from the way he was now, but it still seemed odd to think she could have met him all those years ago...

'I should have realised.' She shook her head self-derisively.

Peter smiled. 'Jonas was wild in those days,' he recalled, as if he could guess her thoughts of a few minutes ago. 'He was into everything. Fast cars. Drink. Women.' His face became shadowed again. 'It's ironic really that it was a woman who once again split the family apart. Lucy might have been made in Claire's image,' he said grimly. 'A young, slightly less knowing Claire. Maybe that was what attracted Jonas to her. God knows what Charles saw in her!' He shook his head disgustedly.

Cassandra had gone very still, her heart pounding loudly in her ears. A woman. Charles and Jonas had fallen out over a woman? A girl really. It had never occurred to her that might be the reason... Although she remembered Jonas's bitterness now about the one time he had been in love, and also Peter's comments to Jonas on Christmas Day concerning his reasons for marrying her.

'Charles took Lucy away from Jonas,' she realised dully. Here lay Jonas's real reason for wanting to marry her. It had nothing to do with her father or those shares, and everything to do with revenge for what Charles had done to Jonas all those years ago. She felt ill...

'Not quite,' Peter answered drily, not seeming to have noticed how pale Cassandra had become, her eyes haunted, the dark shadows beneath them appearing even darker, her cheeks hollow. 'Lucy just decided Charles, as the older, already established brother, was a much surer bet than the fiery but as yet unproved Jonas. She and Jonas had been dating for several months, but within a week of being introduced to Charles Lucy was chasing after him unashamedly.'

But Charles hadn't had to be caught! And he had never mentioned this girl Lucy to her. Oh, Cassandra hadn't expected him to confess to every relationship from his past; after all, he was a lot older than her, and of course there had been other women. But this girl Lucy had been Jonas's girlfriend first, and was the cause of the bad feeling between the two brothers; Charles should have told Cassandra about her.

Had Charles not told her about Lucy because he had known how disappointed she would have been in his behaviour? She had known that same disappointment in him so many times during their marriage that it was a wonder she could still be surprised—or hurt—by anything he had done. But she was...

'What happened—happened, Cassandra.' Peter was looking at her regretfully as he saw the pained disillusionment in the paleness of her face.

What had 'happened' had almost destroyed Jonas! She could see it all now. In Lucy, Jonas had at last believed he had found someone of his own to love, someone who would love him in return, for himself. He had chosen badly, and Lucy had betrayed him with his own brother, the worst possible thing that could have happened.

Good God, no wonder Jonas was so successful in business; he had had a burning fury driving him on all these years, a need to prove to his father, Charles, and Lucy that he didn't need any of them. That he didn't need anyone...

Her expression was bleak now as she looked across at Peter. 'And Lucy? What happened to her?'

He shrugged. 'Charles hadn't been as blind to what she was like as I had initially thought; apparently, he made it clear to her that he wasn't offering the marriage that Jonas had been thinking of. And so she tried to go back to Jonas.' Peter shook his head. 'He wasn't interested in her any more, of course——'

'Can you blame him for feeling that way?' Cassandra choked, only able to imagine the humiliation Jonas must have gone through when the woman he loved seemed to prefer his older brother. It was also the reason Jonas was so determined now to marry Charles's widow; it must seem like ironic justice in his eyes. And Jonas got so much more than revenge on Charles for what he had done by marrying her, of course...

'No,' Peter grimaced. 'Of course I can't blame him for that. But Charles actually did him a favour——'

'Jonas didn't see it that way!' she snapped knowingly. She knew Jonas that well, at least!

Peter shook his head. 'There was the most unholy row, with the result that Jonas finally stormed out, telling us he didn't want anything from us in future, that he—he had never really belonged to this family anyway, that he would make a life for himself elsewhere, where no one knew this damned family!' He sighed. 'And from the look of him he has succeeded in doing just that.'

Cassandra swallowed hard. 'He appears to have done, yes,' she agreed guardedly, still trying to take in all that she had been told today, and what she could do to change things between herself and Jonas. There had to be something.

'Professionally successful,' his father nodded understandingly. 'On a personal level he's still very bitter. I have no idea what sort of life he's led these past twelve years or so, Cassandra.' He looked at her frowningly. 'I knew where he had gone, of course, tried to contact him several times in the beginning, but it was all rejected. I hoped that, given time and maturity, he would perhaps see things differently, grow to understand—— When he came back earlier this year it was the first time I had seen him for twelve years.' His thoughts were inward now, again remembering. 'He's grown into a fine figure of a man, tall and strong, tough but usually fair in business from what I've heard of his dealings over the years.'

It was ironic that Charles had been the one to bring Jonas back to England, by leaving him those shares in Hunter and Kyle. And by doing so he had put her completely at Jonas's mercy...!

'Tough but usually fair in business' was the reputation Peter had heard of his younger son; but Jonas was being anything but fair in his dealings with her! She knew what she had to do now, and both dreaded and anticipated the outcome.

'Those photographs, Peter,' she prompted briskly, seeing how lost in the sad memories the old man had now become, and knowing that brooding about all of this again now wasn't going to help him. Or Jonas. 'I'd like to see them now if you know where they are.'

Peter had albums of photographs, hundreds of them of ancestors, and his own children. Cassandra supposed, thinking back to those early days with Charles, that she must have seen some of these photographs before; Peter had taken great delight, she remembered, at the beginning of her engagement to Charles, in showing her youthfully embarrassing photographs of him, from lying naked on a rug as a baby to being slightly overweight in his early teens. She had taken little notice at the time of the other dark-eyed little boy also in some of those photographs, having little interest at the time in the younger brother whom she hadn't met and was never likely to meet either.

This second child was easily recognisable as Jonas, although his hair had been longer and curly then, not kept in that severely short style he now favoured. The dark eyes that looked up out of the photographs had always seemed older than their years, rarely reflecting the humour of his laughing mouth, his expression more often than not broodingly grave, even from early childhood. Cassandra's heart went out to the bewildered little boy he had become after the break-up of his parents' marriage.

There were photographs of Claire Hunter too, kept, Cassandra felt sure, only for the benefit of the child she had done her best to poison against his father and older brother; Peter obviously didn't need any photographic reminders of his second wife! Cassandra had no idea what the other woman looked like nowadays, but then she had been beautiful, tall and dark, elegantly slender, every feature perfect, from her delicately arched black brows, aqua-blue eyes, tiny nose, to her poutingly lovely mouth.

'A word of warning—beware of Claire when you meet her.' Peter was also looking at the photograph of the woman he had made his second wife, Jonas's mother. 'Those delicate little teeth have a vicious bite,' he grated harshly.

'It may not come to that,' Cassandra dismissed dully, knowing already that she wasn't going to like Claire Hunter, that she couldn't feel comfortable with a woman who could do to her child what Claire had so selfishly done to Jonas.

Peter looked across at Cassandra frowningly. 'But I thought Jonas was adamant about inviting her to the wedding...?' He looked puzzled.

'He is,' Cassandra dismissed vaguely, not wanting to get into an in-depth conversation now about why there was a possibility that she and Claire would never meet. 'Peter, could I borrow a couple of these photographs to take away with me?' she requested briskly.

'Yes, of course. But——'

'I'll make sure you get them back,' she promised, taking the photographs she wanted, knowing exactly which ones they were.

Peter still watched her with puzzled eyes. 'Cassandra, what do you intend doing with them?' His gaze followed her as she stood up.

She reached out to squeeze his shoulder reassuringly. 'I'm not sure yet,' she admitted truthfully. 'What I do know is there's a hurt little boy in Jonas who needs to come out. The pain has to be faced, accepted, and then lived with, not left to fester and grow.'

'And you think those photographs might help?' Peter didn't look convinced.

'I don't honestly know,' she admitted wearily. 'All I do know is that someone has to try.'

His eyes widened admiringly. 'You do love Jonas.'

'Very much,' she nodded. 'Too much to let this continue.' She didn't enlarge on what 'this' was. 'Take care, Peter. I'll be in touch.'

'I hope so,' he nodded, a deep sadness in his eyes. 'I truly hope so.'

She hoped so too. But despite what she had said to Peter, she wasn't in the least confident about what she intended doing...

She knew her next meeting with Jonas wasn't going to be a particularly friendly one, when she arrived at her mother's house to pick up Bethany and discovered Jonas had already been there and had driven her daughter home!

'Where the hell have you been all afternoon?'

Cassandra had delayed going into the sitting-room, where she knew Jonas waited, only long enough to go down to the kitchen where Bethany was being given her tea by Jean, to assure herself that Bethany had enjoyed herself at her grandmother's this afternoon and that she was now being fed; as her young daughter was now eating her favourite tea of chips and fish-fingers Cassandra knew her presence was superfluous while she ate it!

But Cassandra was in no hurry to go upstairs to the sitting-room either, could feel Jonas's presence there like a powerful force to be reckoned with.

Nevertheless, she knew the longer she delayed, the more angry he was likely to become, and as he and Bethany had already been back at the house half an hour he was probably angry enough!

He stood over by the large bay window when she entered the room, hands thrust into the pockets of his suit trousers, broodingly unapproachable in the darkly formal clothing and snowy white shirt, a blue silk tie knotted severely at his throat.

He had come to the house here first this evening, Jean had informed her, and from the look of him that had been straight after his business meeting had finished. He had only gone on to her mother's after Jean had told him they had gone there for the afternoon; Cassandra had told Jean that was where she was going, hadn't wanted the other woman to have to lie for her if Jonas should telephone in her absence. It was Joy, apparently, who had felt no compunction about telling Jonas that Cassandra had only stayed long enough to drop Bethany off at the house, before going off on some mysterious business of her own. Joy could get awards for stirring up trouble—and enjoying doing it!

Not that Cassandra had intended keeping her visit to Peter as a secret from Jonas; in the circumstances she could hardly do that. But she had been going to tell him in her own time, in her own way. Now she wasn't going to be given the chance to do that!

'Jonas,' she greeted him lightly, softly closing the door behind her. 'Thank you for collecting Bethany from my mother's for me——'

'Don't act the polite innocent with me, Cassandra,' he cut in harshly, striding purposefully across the room to glare down at her. 'I asked you where you had been all afternoon. If it was with that young puppy Simeon——'

'Don't be ridiculous, Jonas.' It was her turn to snap now, facing him unflinchingly. 'And why do you persist in calling him a puppy? He's older than me, not some adolescent. And as he's my assistant,' she hurried on as she saw the storm clouds increase at her defence of Simeon, 'I would have been perfectly justified in my need to see him.'

'And did you need to see him this afternoon?' Jonas's mouth twisted derisively.

Coming from any other man this behaviour could be thought to be that of a jealous lover, but from Jonas it was obviously intended as yet another insult to emphasise what he already believed of her.

Cassandra ignored it, knowing that to allow herself to become as angry as he was certainly wasn't the answer; besides, she was desperately trying to come up with a way of answering him without making his anger worse! Once she had told him it was his father she had been to see this afternoon, and not Simeon, then the whole truth of her visit would have to come out. And, angry as Jonas already was, that wouldn't achieve anything. Would she be wiser telling him it *had* been Simeon she had been to see, bear the wrath that would follow that, and then talk to him about the things his father had told her when he was in a more reasonable frame of mind? If Jonas ever was in a more reasonable frame of mind!

'What sort of mother are you, anyway?' Jonas attacked before she could make any reply, reaching out to shake her, taking the matter completely out of her control as he threw the next accusation at her. 'Dumping your child at your mother's while you sneak off to meet some man——'

'I didn't sneak off to meet some man,' she returned heatedly, stung by both the aspersions he was casting on her ability to be a good mother to Bethany and this obsession he seemed to have of there being a relationship between her and Simeon.

Jonas's hands bit painfully into her upper arms, his harshly hewn features only inches away from her now as he glowered down at her. 'How long has this affair with your assistant been going on anyway?' he demanded viciously.

'I told you——'

'Even while Charles was alive?' he continued remorselessly. 'Did you deceive your much older husband even then with your young lover?' he accused disgustedly.

'Don't judge me as having the same standards as your mother——' She broke off as soon as she realised what she had said, staring up at Jonas now with widely apprehensive eyes, her face gone deathly white.

Jonas was very still, a nerve pulsing in his tightly clenched jaw, his eyes dark, his hands falling slowly back to his sides as he released his grip on her arms. 'What did you say?' he said softly.

Dangerously softly.

Oh, God...!

CHAPTER NINE

CASSANDRA hadn't meant—hadn't wanted—— So much
for biding her time, talking to Jonas about the past in
a way that would rationalise it all. She shouldn't have
allowed herself to react to that taunt about her cheating
on Charles during their marriage, because that was all
it had been—a vicious taunt on Jonas's part because he
was furiously angry with her for disappearing in that
way without telling him where she was going.

The expression in Jonas's eyes had gone dead now,
icily, coldly dead, as he moved away from her, his face
harshly forbidding. Cassandra felt a shiver of apprehension down her spine. If she had thought him arrogantly cruel in the past, she now realised how wrong she
had been; Jonas looked capable of ripping her to pieces
with a few well-chosen words at this moment!

She put a hand out towards him, not daring actually
to touch him, sure he would snap completely if she did
that. 'Jonas——'

'You went to see my father,' he stated flatly, ignoring
that beseeching hand she held out to him.

Cassandra swallowed hard, knowing she had handled
this all wrong—oh, so very wrong! 'Yes,' she acknowledged with simple honesty, her arm falling back against
her side, her hands trembling slightly.

'After I specifically asked you not to do——'

'You *told* me, Jonas,' she corrected gently. 'You never *ask* for anything.' Some of the colour returned to her cheeks as she remembered that he had asked when they were making love; he had pleaded with her then, as she had pleaded with him. But the man who had made love to her was as far removed from this man as fire from ice. Although fire melted ice . . . Not this time, she knew; Jonas was too chillingly furious right now to be melted by anything she did or said! And thinking about the time they had made love wasn't going to help her now!

Jonas scowled darkly. 'You knew I didn't want you to go there,' he grated accusingly.

She gave a ruefully acknowledging movement at that. 'But I didn't at any time say that I wouldn't go,' she reminded him. In fact, she had carefully changed the subject that day so that she couldn't be pushed into agreeing to something she knew she couldn't do; she had known she had to see Peter.

'No,' Jonas accepted hardly, 'you didn't do that.' His mouth twisted. 'So now you consider yourself an expert on the family history—my family history!' he taunted, although his cheeks were flushed in agitation.

Cassandra drew in a deep breath, choosing her words carefully this time, not wanting to exacerbate the situation any more. If that were possible. 'I merely asked your father——'

'And he merely told you!' Jonas accused, glaring. 'If you had wanted to know anything about my past then you should have damn well asked me!'

She raised dark brows. 'And you would have told me?' she prompted in quiet scepticism, doing her best to remain calm in the face of his fury—even if she was actually quaking in her shoes at the expectation of the explosion she was sure was still to come. Thank God the knocking of her knees was hidden beneath the length of her skirt!

'A damn sight less biased version, yes!' he nodded curtly.

She drew in a ragged breath. 'Your father has his own memories of what happened——'

'They aren't the same as mine!' Jonas flared gratingly.

'Of course they aren't.' She attempted to soothe the situation. 'You were a child, and Claire was your mother.' She shrugged.

'I did not imagine the way I remember my mother!' he scorned dismissively.

'I'm not saying you did, Jonas, I just—— Let's look at today for an example,' she reasoned determinedly. 'In your eyes I "dumped" my child on my mother for the afternoon while I "went off" to meet someone. In Bethany's eyes I took her to visit her grandmother, where she was thoroughly spoilt all afternoon—and then had the added treat of being driven home by her favourite man! The adult and child's point of view, Jonas, and so completely different.' Cassandra looked at him challengingly, wondering how he was going to defend his child's view of his mother's actions without at the same time admitting he had been wrong to attack her in the way he had over Bethany; no doubt he would manage it somehow!

'That was different——'

'Not at all.' Cassandra insisted. 'Your father told me about his marriage to your mother from the side of the unhappy husband, you judged me this afternoon from

the point of view of the outraged fiancé; not so very
different after all.' She raised her brows pointedly. 'The
truth lies somewhere in the middle, I would think.' Which
still left Claire Hunter as a sad excuse for a mother, as
far as Cassandra was concerned; what other sort of
mother could possibly have tried to poison her child
against his father and brother?

Jonas looked at her with narrowed eyes. 'What exactly
did my father tell you about his marriage to my mother?'

Careful, Cassandra, she warned herself again; Jonas
was obviously very sensitive where his mother was concerned. 'From what I can tell they were unsuited——'

'Unsuited!' Jonas scorned disgustedly. 'My father kept
thrusting the virtues of his saintly Kathleen down my
mother's throat until she choked on her damned
perfection!'

Cassandra had already guessed some of that, had
realised Peter should never have remarried at all when
he still loved his first wife the way he did, that it must
have been an almost impossible situation for Claire to
have married into. But at the same time the answer to
the problem surely hadn't been to turn her son against
his own family and take a string of lovers for herself.
The fact that she had done the latter explained why Jonas
had reacted so violently after *they* made love when he
had thought she had been thinking of Charles! Jonas
might not be willing to accept the fact, but his mother's
behaviour had coloured all of his life.

And, as she had already pointed out to Jonas, the
truth of the past surely lay somewhere in between the
memories he and Peter had of it.

She nodded. 'I'm sure they would be among the first to admit they made a mistake——'

'My father, admit he made a mistake?' Jonas derided harshly. 'You obviously don't know him very well.'

She didn't pretend to know Peter well; their conversation today had been the longest and most intimate they had ever shared. But what she did know after talking to him today, no matter what had or hadn't happened in the past, was that Peter loved his youngest son as much as he had loved Charles, that the strain that had existed in their relationship had caused him a lot of pain over the years, a pain perhaps Jonas couldn't fully understand because he had never been a father himself.

'I don't pretend to,' she acknowledged gently. 'I do know he wished things were different between the two of you——'

'Is that why he once denied even being my father?' Jonas challenged with distaste.

Cassandra frowned. And then she remembered what Peter had said about the custody case over Jonas, how *Claire* had been the one to tell the court Peter wasn't Jonas's father, in an effort to win the case for herself. Surely the other woman hadn't twisted that around to make it look as if Peter was denying his own son? There had been no reason to tell Jonas anything about that at all, except as a means of justifying her own actions at some future date. What sort of mother was Claire Hunter?

'And yet he was the one to get custody of you, Jonas,' Cassandra pointed out softly, knowing by the paleness of Jonas's cheeks that he was well aware of how unusual it was for a father to attain custody of a child, let alone a father who had supposedly denied even being the father!

'Yes,' he admitted harshly now. 'Once it was proved to him that he had to be my father, then there was no way he was going to let me go and live with my mother!' He shook his head. 'He may seem like a harmless, lonely old man now, Cassandra, but he wasn't then,' he remembered bitterly. 'He didn't want me, but he wasn't about to let my mother have me either!'

'That doesn't explain why she more or less ignored your existence for the next few years,' Cassandra pointed out gently.

'My father made it virtually impossible for her to see me,' he defended harshly.

Claire Hunter had such a lot to answer for! 'Did you ever talk to your father about any of this, Jonas?' she prompted with a frown.

'Talk to him?' Jonas began to pace the room. 'What was the point of that? Then I would just have to listen to the same lies you did today,' he scorned. 'How gullible you are, Cassandra; I would never have believed it of you!'

No, because it was easier for him to believe all women were as fickle as that girl Lucy had been. Except his mother, of course, when in actual fact it had been his mother who had really formed his early distrust of a woman's honesty. If he hadn't already been influenced by her behaviour then he probably wouldn't have reacted with such emotional violence to Lucy's betrayal, would have taken it all as part of life's disappointments, of growing up. Not that Jonas could see that. Perhaps he never would...

Cassandra knew that she didn't even want to meet Claire Hunter, wasn't sure she would be able to contain her anger at what the other woman had deliberately and maliciously done to her son in an effort to hit out at his father and brother.

'Not gullible, Jonas,' she denied sadly. 'I just perhaps have more of an open mind on the subject than you do.'

His mouth thinned. 'We're never going to agree on that subject, so we may as well forget about it,' he dismissed harshly. 'What else did he tell you?' His gaze had narrowed on her speculatively. 'I can't believe he stopped there.'

She didn't have to tell him about Charles being the one to transfer Hunter and Kyle funds; in fact she knew she should avoid it at all costs just now. But it couldn't wait until after the wedding; it had to be before then, all secrets between them—on her side at least!—out in the open. She wouldn't become yet another woman to have deceived him, no matter what he might believe to the contrary. There had to be time in the next four days to tell him the truth about that. There had to be!

She moistened her lips with the tip of her tongue, instantly noticing the way Jonas's eyes darkened at the movement, her eyes widening at this obvious reaction. He hadn't so much as attempted to touch her in an intimate way since they made love on Christmas Day, had meant it when he told her he wouldn't make love to her again, and yet from his reaction to her now he certainly wasn't as immune to her physically as he wanted her to believe he was. It was a start. She was desperate enough to grasp at any straw!

'What's the matter, Cassandra?' Jonas derided hardly as she continued to hesitate. 'Can't you even talk about the fact that your precious Charles wasn't so damned perfect after all, that he wasn't above poaching his own brother's girlfriend?'

'I never believed he was,' she said quietly. Never that! 'Your father told me about Lucy,' she acknowledged dully.

His mouth twisted. 'Not such a paragon after all, hmm?' he scorned. 'It would appear Charles always had a weakness for girls young enough to be his daughter; Lucy was only twenty to his thirty-six!'

This was yet another deliberate taunt to wound, Cassandra knew, because she had forced him to talk of his mother in a way he couldn't accept. But the fact that she knew that didn't make his gibe hurt any the less, and she felt herself flinch at the barb.

She was disappointed in Charles's behaviour all those years ago, she couldn't pretend she wasn't, but it all happened long before she had a relationship with Charles. And the truth about Charles was 'something in between' too; he wasn't perfect, as she and Peter knew only too well, despite what Jonas believed to the contrary! He had simply been human, with human failings.

She drew in a ragged breath. 'Despite what you might like to think, Jonas,' she told him steadily, 'Charles and I understood each other.'

'He wanted me to be his best man at your wedding, you know,' Jonas scorned dismissively.

'Yes, I did know,' she acknowledged quietly. 'We obviously discussed it before Charles asked you.'

Jonas nodded abruptly. 'As olive-branches went, it was like a slap in the face!'

Cassandra could see, with hindsight, that perhaps it might have seemed that way to Jonas, and yet she believed in her own mind that Charles—insensitive again, but that was his only sin, she was sure—hadn't meant it that way, that he had genuinely thought, if Jonas had accepted, that the family might at last become reunited. Although he might perhaps have chosen a better, less painful way to have invited Jonas back into the family!

'Talking of weddings...' Jonas looked pointedly at his wristwatch. 'We're due at the church ourselves in just over an hour. Do you know if Joy and Colin have remembered the rehearsal? I didn't have a chance to discuss it with Colin earlier today.'

Cassandra knew that he was deliberately changing the subject, that he had decided he didn't want to discuss any more of this just now. She didn't feel up to battling her way through any more confrontational conversations herself just now, but at the same time she knew their conversation was far from over...

She gave a rueful grimace. 'Joy is looking forward to it, I know!' As Joy and Colin were their two witnesses it was essential they be at the rehearsal this evening.

Jonas laughed softly. 'I'm sure she is. You and your sister aren't very much alike, are you?' he drawled.

Cassandra looked at him sharply. 'What's that supposed to mean?'

He arched dark brows at her defensive reaction. 'It wasn't meant as a criticism,' he murmured mockingly—implying the opposite!

Just exactly what had he meant by the remark? It was true, she and Joy weren't alike; in fact they were completely unalike; Joy, for one thing, would never have allowed herself to be blackmailed into this situation in the first place! Joy would simply have told Jonas what he could do with his threats, and damn the outcome.

Not for the first time, Cassandra wished she had her sister's self-absorbed determination. If she had she might not have been so vulnerable to Jonas's demands. Had Jonas realised that? Was that why she had been the one he had chosen to pressurise into marriage? He said it was because of Bethany too, but she couldn't help wondering now how true that was...!

Her eyes blazed deeply golden as she glared at him. 'The same could be said of you and Charles!' Her remark was deliberately provoking, and she knew by the narrowing of his eyes to steely slits, and the way his mouth tightened into a thin line, that her barb had also hit home. 'I'll meet you at the church, shall I?' she added brightly, her eyes deceptively innocent.

Jonas looked at her consideringly for a moment. 'Maybe not so different from Joy after all...' he murmured hardly. 'And Jean is preparing an early dinner for us here,' he added. 'So we can go to the church together later.'

Cassandra was stung that he had once again taken over her home, although at the same time she realised it was something she was going to have to get used to once she and Jonas were married. Not that they intended staying on in this house for long after they were married; Jonas had tersely informed her that he was willing to make do for the moment, would use the room next to hers that

Charles had used as a dressing-room, but that one of the first things they were going to do in the New Year was look for a house of their own.

It was going to be a wrench for Cassandra to leave here, and Bethany had known no other home, but even putting the way Jonas felt about Charles to one side— if that were possible!—then moving into the house of your wife's first husband wasn't an ideal arrangement at the best of times.

But once again this was something Jonas had told her was going to happen; he hadn't actually asked for her opinion! Her mouth twisted mockingly. 'This isn't to be a complete rehearsal, then, with the bride and groom arriving separately?'

Jonas met her gaze steadily. 'If it were I would also be sharing your bed later tonight—and I have no intention of doing that!'

Cassandra paled at the intended insult. Why did she bother trying to fence verbally with this man? She always lost! Although perhaps, in the circumstances, where of her going to see Peter without Jonas's knowledge was concerned, perhaps she had got off lightly. For the moment...

Her mother and Godfrey were present at the rehearsal too, with Bethany bobbing about excitedly, wanting to know everything that was going on.

It was a nightmare for Cassandra, this church blessing nothing like the cold formality of the register office ceremony which the registrar had taken them through briefly when they went to see him. The blessing was almost like the church ceremony, only a few of the words changed to allow for the fact that she and Jonas would already be married when they entered the church. The beautiful solemnity of the service brought home to Cassandra yet again exactly what she was taking on marrying a man whom she loved but who didn't love her.

In fact, she was in somewhat of a daze when the vicar came over to talk to them jovially after the rehearsal, a kindly man with twinkling blue eyes and snowy white hair, a man who would be totally shocked and dismayed if he were to know the truth behind this marriage!

Jonas kept up a light conversation with the older man, although the tight hold he had of Cassandra's arm told her he was well aware of just how close she was to panicking completely and dashing out of the church and away from this marriage—and damn the consequences!

She couldn't help the way she felt, just felt totally shaken by the whole thing, almost collapsing with relief once they were at last able to go, hardly aware of taking her leave of her family to get in the car beside Jonas, Bethany in the back.

Jonas was grim-faced on that drive back to the house, and the harshness of his mood promised retribution once they were alone—which wasn't long after they arrived back, Bethany being more than ready for her bed by this time, Jean absenting herself too once she had brought them a tray of coffee through to the sitting-room.

'For God's sake snap out of it,' Jonas rasped as he glared down at Cassandra, hands thrust deep into his trouser pockets. 'You've looked like a ghost ever since we entered the church!' He scowled at the memory.

She swallowed hard. 'I'm just glad that part, at least, is over.' Although what she was going to feel like on the actual wedding day, if she felt this ill after only the rehearsal, she dreaded to think!

He gave a harsh snort. 'I'm sure your mother will be even more pleased once the actual wedding is over!'

'My mother...?' Cassandra looked up at him sharply. 'What on earth do you mean by that?' It had been too sarcastically put not to have some sort of hidden meaning.

'Isn't it obvious, Cassandra?' Jonas drawled mockingly. 'Your mother obviously realises that once the two of us are married the family secret will be safely buried at last!' he insisted scathingly.

'Family secret...?' Cassandra repeated again dazedly, starting to feel like a burbling idiot. But she didn't understand—— Oh, yes, she did; her cheeks coloured hotly. 'I doubt very much my mother even knows about—about that!' she told him heatedly.

Good God, he was making it difficult, with his continued ridiculing of her father, for her not to tell him it had been his brother and not her father who had diverted that money! It was only the fact that Charles had also been her husband that kept her from angrily hurling the information at him.

He raised dark brows, his tension having abated slightly now that he had succeeded in angering her, back in control of the situation again. 'I had the impression your parents had quite a close marriage...?'

'They did,' she confirmed with a frown. 'But what does that——?' If they had that close a marriage her father would have told her mother what he had done. As Charles had confided in her. Eventually.

Did her mother know the truth anyway? Did she, as Cassandra had so briefly suspected the night of her mother's dinner party, know exactly what had happened to company funds?

Her father had always discussed business with her mother when he got in from the office, and what Charles had done had affected them all, been so enormous that—— Good God, did her mother know? Was that why she had thrust Joy at Jonas when he first came back to England, been so obviously disappointed when it became obvious he wasn't interested in her, and then so relieved again when it turned out that Cassandra was to marry him instead? Was that why her mother had been so jumpy two weeks ago, so determined to draw Jonas into their family circle? Had she hoped he would be less inclined to take action if there was that bond? If that was the case, then it opened up all sorts of questions Cassandra would like answers to...!

Jonas's mouth twisted derisively. 'You didn't seriously think your mother was so pleased about our marriage because she actually approves of me?' he taunted, shaking his head pityingly. 'I'm the last thing she wants in a son-in-law.'

And Charles—what had her mother thought of him as a son-in-law once she knew what he had done, how close to ruin he had brought the company? To her credit, her mother had said nothing, but that didn't mean she hadn't thought plenty of things!

'Not after Golden Boy Charles,' Jonas added scornfully.

'For God's sake stop calling him that!' Cassandra snapped. 'Are you so steeped in bitterness that you can't see, for all their faults, your brother and your father loved you, that it was your mother who lied to you all these years——?'

'I told you earlier to leave her out of this!' he rasped angrily.

'Why should I?' she said exasperatedly. 'Are you frightened to talk to your father, Jonas? Is that it——?'

'I'm not frightened of anyone, least of all him!' his voice rose furiously.

'Then prove it,' she challenged impatiently. 'Go to your father, listen to what he has to say, and then, if you still feel the same way about him, fine. But don't base what you're saying to me on prejudices that are over twenty years old! As for Charles——' she was breathing deeply in her agitation '—I know he isn't completely blameless——'

'That's big of you!' Jonas scorned sneeringly.

'Oh, shut up, will you? Just shut up!' She glared across at him. 'It was Charles who was responsible for diverting company funds, not my father!' It all came out in a rush now that she had finally found the courage to say it, although she fell into a stunned silence once the truth was out.

There was a heavy silence from Jonas too after her outburst, a tension-filled few minutes when he looked at her as if she had gone completely mad. And then he spoke. 'What the hell are you talking about, Cassandra?' he demanded impatiently. 'Of course it wasn't Charles. He——'

'But it was, Jonas,' she insisted desperately; the last thing she had expected was that he wouldn't believe her!

'I let you go on thinking it was my father because—well, because——'

'Cassandra, I can assure you I made sure of my facts before I even spoke to you on the subject—all my facts,' he insisted gratingly. 'And, I can assure you, Charles's name was not on the relevant documents. But your father's certainly was!'

Cassandra had been on the point of tears, feeling as if she had betrayed Charles, but now she could only stare up at Jonas disbelievingly, knowing by the scathing expression on his face that he really believed what he was saying was the truth.

What did it mean? How had her father's name got on to those documents? Unless he *had* been the one responsible, after all...

'What the hell are you hoping to achieve with this, Cassandra?' Jonas challenged harshly now. 'Your father was the one responsible; I can assure you of that. Who it was is actually irrelevant—the outcome is still the same: you are going to become my wife in four days' time!'

It wasn't irrelevant to her. Why had Charles lied to her? Why?

'And you had damn well better get used to the idea,' Jonas added viciously, pulling her roughly to her feet before grinding his mouth down on hers. Cassandra was too numbed by this time to offer any sort of reaction at all, either for or against the onslaught.

His expression was even more savage when he at last raised his head from hers. 'There's going to be no escape, Cassandra, no last-minute reprieve.' His eyes glittered down at her. 'You *will* be my wife!' He thrust her away from him before striding out of the room and then out of the house, the front door closing with controlled violence behind him.

Cassandra didn't move from the spot where he had left her, couldn't move, not even if her life had depended upon it. And in a way it did, because if she couldn't convince Jonas that she had thought she was telling him the truth just now about Charles and her father, then her life as his wife was going to be a living nightmare!

CHAPTER TEN

HER mother looked surprised to see her, but her reaction was understandable in the circumstances; Cassandra had given no indication when they parted earlier that she intended visiting her later this evening. And it was late, after ten. But Cassandra knew she had to see her mother tonight, that this couldn't wait until morning.

She had sat at home in stunned dismay long after Jonas had left so abruptly, going over and over in her mind what he had told her. It was her father, after all, not Charles. It was her father, after all, *not* Charles. No matter how many times she chased the thoughts round and round in her head, she still came back to that basic fact. And Jonas was so sure, so very sure of this being the correct version that there was no way she could doubt it any more.

After agonising over why Charles should have told her it had been him and not her father who had been involved, she could come up with only one solution: his own weaknesses aside—or because of them!—Charles had wanted to spare her the painful disillusionment of learning that her dead father, the father she had openly adored, had left things in such a mess. Charles couldn't have guessed he would be dead himself within two months of the older man's death, the problem unresolved.

Then she had sat and cried for the depth of Charles's caring, knowing it had to have been his way of making up for his own inadequacies during their marriage, inadequacies he had been just too lazy, or incapable, of doing anything about...

But once the tears had finally ceased she had realised that Jonas had to be right about her mother too—that she had to have known the truth all along. And this visit Cassandra was paying to her now was long overdue!

'Is something wrong?' Her mother put aside the book she had been reading to stand up, her expression anxious. 'Bethany...?'

'She's safely tucked up in bed asleep, and Jean is listening out for her,' Cassandra easily assured her, her gaze fixed steadily on her mother as she took the time to remove her coat and gloves and throw them over the back of a chair; she had a feeling this wasn't going to be a quick visit.

Marguerite looked relieved at hearing Bethany was all right, although she still looked puzzled, starting to shift uncomfortably under the steadiness of Cassandra's gaze. 'What is it, Cassandra?' she finally snapped irritably. 'You and Jonas haven't rowed again, have you?'

Was it her imagination, or had her mother's anxiety returned at this suggestion? No, she was sure she hadn't imagined that little flicker of alarm in her mother's eyes, her sudden tension, at the thought of an alienated Jonas.

'No, Jonas and I haven't argued,' she told her wearily. 'No more than usual, anyway,' she added drily; after all, tonight was far from the first time Jonas had stormed out in a temper. But he would be back; she didn't doubt that. He had to be. He had meant it when he told her she would become his wife in four days' time.

'You and Jonas do seem to have rather a—tempestuous relationship,' her mother acknowledged ruefully. 'But some people do, of course, and it seems to work out well for them. So I shouldn't worry too much——'

'Mother, stop burbling,' Cassandra cut in calmly. 'Jonas wants to marry me only because he wants the shares in the company Daddy left me, and control over the ones Charles left Bethany,' she told her mother bluntly. 'Whether our marriage works or not will be completely irrelevant to the arrangement, so I can assure you I'm not worrying about that part of things at all!'

Her mother's gasp of astonishment seemed genuine enough. 'I'm sure you're wrong about this, Cassandra——'

'I'm not,' she returned tautly, dropping down into one of the armchairs. 'You may as well sit down too, Mother,' she advised softly. 'We have a lot to talk about, and we may as well be comfortable while we do it. Sit down, Mother!' she repeated sharply when Marguerite didn't attempt to move.

Blue eyes widened indignantly, but, for all that, this time her mother sat. 'I must say, Cassandra——' she straightened her skirt with agitated movements '—that I'm not particularly happy with the way you're talking to me this evening!'

Her mouth twisted wryly. 'I've been taking lessons from Jonas,' she dismissed drily.

'A certain amount of forcefulness can be an attractive trait in a man,' her mother told her primly. 'But in a woman it's just not——'

'You're burbling again, Mother,' Cassandra told her with raised brows. 'Which is most *unattractive* in a man *or* a woman!'

Delicate colour darkened cheeks already tinted with blusher. 'After that slightly rebellious time in your teens when you were so determined over what you were going to do with your life, I had thought you had become my quieter, more respectful daughter,' her mother began in a reproving voice—obviously striving to regain *some* control of this conversation at least!

Cassandra wasn't in the least cowed by the rebuke, her eyes narrowed. 'Is that why you were so relieved when Jonas passed over Joy and decided to marry me instead?' she challenged softly. 'Because you believed I would be the more compliant——?'

'Cassandra, have you been drinking?' Her mother frowned.

'I only wish I had!' she said self-derisively. 'Maybe then none of this would matter to me. You didn't answer my question, Mother.' She wasn't blind to the way her mother had tried to change the subject. 'Did you think I would be more compliant than Joy would ever have been, once the truth came out?'

Her mother's cheeks lost all colour beneath the blusher now, giving her face a peculiar clownish appearance. 'The truth, Cassandra?' She gave a lightly puzzled laugh—that even to her own ears couldn't have been the success she had wanted! 'What are you talking about? I don't think I'm the one burbling, dear——'

'Don't patronise me, Mother,' Cassandra cut in sharply, anger hardening her voice now. 'What happened? Did Charles come to you and Daddy and tell you he knew about Daddy's transfer of company funds, and then when Daddy died you persuaded Charles not to reveal it had been Daddy who——?'

'That isn't the way it happened at all!' her mother defended heatedly, sitting forward tensely on the edge of her seat. 'It was Charles's idea not to——' She broke off abruptly as she saw by Cassandra's triumphant expression that she had fallen into the trap that had been set for her. 'That wasn't fair, Cassandra,' she said shakily.

Cassandra drew in a ragged breath, shaken now at having her worst fears confirmed. 'No,' she acknowledged with a sigh, feeling almost sorry for her mother now as she looked all of her fifty-two years, her beautiful face ravaged and suddenly old. 'But were you really being fair to me when you didn't come to me and tell me the truth once Charles had died?' she prompted huskily.

'Oh, God, Cassandra, I didn't know what to do, where to turn!' Her mother crumpled completely now. 'The last ten months have been a nightmare,' she shook her head, breathing deeply, 'wondering if Jonas was going to find out what had happened!'

'Was there ever a possibility that he wouldn't, once we came to know him?' she sighed.

'No, I suppose not. But I hoped——'

'Me too.' Cassandra gave a rueful nod. 'But don't you think these last ten months might have been less of a nightmare if we could have faced them together, shown a united front instead of keeping it all to ourselves?' But she knew why her mother couldn't come to her, knew it had to do with what seemed to have been a lifetime problem—that of her mother just not being able to understand her, or know how she was going to react to certain things; she had just never been able to get close to Cassandra in the way she was to her youngest daughter, Joy being a much more open person, whether you liked that openness or not.

'You don't understand just how much of a nightmare it's been for me.' Her mother put up a shaking hand to her brow. 'Godfrey has been pressing me to marry him,' she explained at Cassandra's questioning look. 'And, God help me, things have felt so desperate, I almost considered it!'

If there could be any humour in this situation then this statement—poor Godfrey!—would have been it! But there was nothing in the least amusing about any of this. 'How convenient for you, when it turned out *I'm* to be the sacrifice instead of you—to Jonas!' Cassandra snapped, her eyes flashing deep golden.

'I only meant——' Her mother broke off abruptly as the doorbell rang once again, and she frowned her puzzlement at this second late-night caller. 'Who on earth could that be this time of night...? Unless Joy has forgotten her key again.' She sighed wearily at her youngest daughter's thoughtlessness. 'Cassandra, I would rather we didn't discuss any of this in front of Joy——'

'Mother, she isn't a child any more,' she cut in impatiently. 'Don't you think it's time you stopped protecting her from the truth as if she were one? She's twenty-three years of age, not——'

'It has nothing to do with protecting Joy,' her mother told her fiercely, blue eyes flashing familiarly. 'Joy is a chatter-box; she would tell Colin, at least, all about this. I just happen to think the fewer people that know about this, the better chance we have of it not becoming public——' She looked across the room as the door opened and her housekeeper entered the room, quickly followed by her visitor. 'Jonas...!' she gasped, standing up slowly, fear in her face now as she stared at him striding forcefully into the room.

Cassandra stared at him too, although she wasn't altogether sure how she felt about his unexpected appearance here. She had known he would come back; she just hadn't expected it to be this soon! But what on earth was he doing *here*, of all places?'

'When I went back to the house Jean told me you were here,' he answered her unasked question with his usual economy of words.

But why had he gone back to the house at all? she frowned; he hadn't given the impression, when he'd marched out earlier, that he intended returning that quickly! But as usual she could read nothing from his enigmatic expression, knowing she would just have to wait until he felt ready to tell her. *If* he did. As she knew only too well, Jonas was a law unto himself.

'Thank you, Jenkins,' Marguerite dismissed the butler distractedly while still looking at Jonas. 'That will be all this evening—unless you would like a coffee or something, Jonas...?' she added as a flustered afterthought, her hands tightly clenched together in front of her.

His mouth twisted wryly. 'I can help myself to the "or something",' he said drily with a pointed look at the

decanter of brandy that stood on top of the drinks
cabinet. 'In fact,' he added grimly once the butler had
left the room, 'from the look of the two of you, I think
we could all do with a little drop of "or something",'
and he moved to pour the brown liquid into three glasses.

Cassandra couldn't stand brandy, and she knew her
mother wasn't particularly keen on it either, but if Jonas
said they could do with a drop of it, then they probably
could! Neither of them was prepared to argue with him
anyway, and she and her mother took the glasses of
brandy they were offered, her mother still eyeing Jonas
nervously.

Cassandra eyed him warily too, when, his own glass
of brandy in his hand, he chose to sit on the sofa next
to where she had just sat down, rather than in one of
the available armchairs—— And not at the other end of
the sofa either, a cushion width separating them, as far
away from her as it was possible to be, so that his not
touching her of the last few days—except in his anger
earlier!—could continue. Instead he sat on the cushion
next to hers, the weight of his body tipping her slightly
towards him, so that the length of their thighs was
pressed close together, their arms brushing too as he
raised the brandy glass to his lips and drank down a
large swallow of the alcohol with hardly a wince.

'You were saying, when I arrived, ladies...?' He
looked at them both blandly.

Marguerite took a desperate swallow of her own
brandy, almost choking as the fiery liquid hit the back
of her throat!

How much of her mother's last comment had he overheard as he followed the housekeeper down the hallway

to this room? Cassandra wondered. What did it really matter how much he had heard? He had to be made to realise now that she had been telling what she had believed to be the truth, when she told him earlier that Charles was the guilty one. And only her mother, it seemed, could verify that for her.

She looked across at her mother, whose face was slightly flushed again now from the brandy she had almost choked on. 'Tell him,' Cassandra invited quietly.

Her mother swallowed hard. 'Really, Cassandra, I don't think we need trouble Jonas with——'

'I'm already troubled, Marguerite,' he put in huskily. 'I'm deeply troubled by the fact that Cassandra has been led to believe it was Charles and not your husband who diverted company funds into a private venture of his own.'

'Jonas, please.' Marguerite gave a delicate shudder. 'You make David sound like a criminal!' she protested.

Cassandra was still staring at Jonas in speechless wonder; he believed her! When he had left her earlier he had treated her claim with scorn and derision, and now, not two hours later, he had changed his mind; what had happened in those intervening two hours to effect this change?

He turned to look at her as he sensed her gaze on him, dark eyes enigmatic, holding her gaze now as he deliberately transferred the brandy glass to his other hand before reaching out and curling his fingers around one of her hands, the pressure of his fingers light and reassuring. Then he turned with that same deliberation, her hand still firmly held in his, and answered her mother. 'He was,' he confirmed softly. 'What your husband did was effectively a criminal act——'

'It was his own money, for goodness' sake!' her mother scorned this claim.

'—a criminal act that, if he had lived, would have been punishable by law,' Jonas continued determinedly.

Marguerite paled. 'You aren't suggesting that David knew that and deliberately——?'

'No, of course I'm not suggesting your husband deliberately caused the accident that killed him,' Jonas dismissed with impatience. 'What I am saying is that if either partner had still been alive, it might have been impossible to even think of covering this up.' He turned to Cassandra as she tensed at his side. 'Don't worry,' he told her almost gently. 'I'm not about to renege on my side of the deal. Although,' he added grimly, 'I am going to release you from your side of it.'

Cassandra gasped, her heart starting to pound so loudly that she thought he must be able to hear it too. 'You don't want my shares any more...?'

His mouth twisted self-derisively. 'Or a wife that hates me.'

She swallowed hard; Jonas no longer wanted to marry her...? Oh, God, she couldn't imagine her life without him now. She *needed* him!

He gave her hand one last squeeze before releasing it, turning grimly back to her mother now. 'I've been forcing your daughter into marrying me, Marguerite,' he revealed sternly. 'And she was willing to make that sacrifice because she loves you all. And Charles,' he added gruffly, giving Cassandra a look that contained apology. 'You must have loved him very much to put up with what I've put you through this last couple of months.' He sighed, shaking his head.

'I did,' she confirmed huskily, still slightly numbed by his sudden change of mind about marrying her. She had been in love with Charles, still loved him, but as it was possible to love a slightly wayward child, someone who needed to be scolded and pampered in varying degrees; she had never felt protected and secure in that love. She loved Jonas for the living, breathing, vital man that he was, but also because she knew, for all his own vulnerability, that he would be the protector, the one who did the caring. And he was releasing her from their engagement... 'Jonas——'

'I can no longer allow you to make that sacrifice,' he continued harshly, a nerve pulsing in his jaw. 'I'm part of this family too; we'll just have to weather the storm together. Not divided, or resentful, but together,' he insisted firmly.

Cassandra was more puzzled than ever by his change of attitude. Jonas had always acted against the family, both his own and hers. And yet he looked totally sincere in his announcement of a united front.

'I took your advice and went to see my father, Cassandra,' he explained in answer to her obvious puzzlement, a wry twist to his lips at the use of the word 'advice'; they both knew she had been too angry at the time for it to have been that! 'It wasn't easy but—well, I think I've gone a long way to making my peace with him. I listened to what he had to say about his relationship with my mother, and accepted, if not agreed, that things aren't always black and white, that sometimes they're just grey.'

Cassandra's eyes were wide. 'But your mother...?'

He grimaced. 'Is no angel. I've known that for years, but—sometimes it takes an outside view to tell you what you've always known.' He sighed heavily.

Cassandra looked at him concernedly, knowing it hadn't been easy for him to hear those things, let alone admit they were true. 'I'm sorry——'

'I'm not.' He gave a half-smile that didn't quite come off. 'Maybe it's better that it's over,' he shrugged. 'I can think of making a life for myself now that doesn't involve some sort of retribution towards my family. Whatever,' he dismissed with a grimace, 'once I've sorted out this mess at Hunter and Kyle perhaps I'll go back to the States and——'

'No!' Cassandra gasped her dismay at the prospect of him leaving, standing up abruptly to look down at him imploringly. 'Jonas, you can't do that!'

'Don't look so worried,' he soothed wryly. 'I won't go until I'm sure Hunter and Kyle is back on its feet——'

'You don't understand, Jonas,' she told him with barely contained urgency. 'I don't want you to go. Me!' she clarified forcefully as he frowned up at her. 'I don't want you to release me from our engagement either. I want—I want——'

Jonas stood up too now, and as they looked at each other the two of them might have been the only ones in the room. 'What do you wànt, Cassandra?' He was watching her almost warily now, as if he both feared and longed for her answer.

Fear? In Jonas? Not fear, exactly, more trepidation, she amended thoughtfully, as if a lot depended upon her answer. And perhaps it did...

And yet still she hesitated about revealing her complete emotional vulnerability to him. Although if Jonas had come here straight from talking to Peter he must be feeling more than slightly emotionally raw himself! 'Bethany would miss you if you went away,' she said gruffly.

Jonas's eyes darkened with an unfathomable emotion, but his expression softened as he thought of the young child. 'I'll miss her too,' he acknowledged huskily. 'Perhaps you'll allow her to come and visit me some time?'

'In America?'

'Yes,' he confirmed gruffly.

Cassandra moistened her lips nervously. 'You and your wife?' She wasn't a hundred per cent certain of the reason he was going back to America, and if it was a woman he was actually returning to...!

His mouth twisted in ruefull self-mockery. 'I doubt I'll ever marry now.'

She looked at him intently, hope soaring in her heart at his use of the word 'now'. 'Why not?'

'Maybe it would be better if I left you two alone to talk?' Her mother stood up, reminding them of her presence, obviously feeling very much in the way.

'It's all right, Mother.' Cassandra was the one to answer her firmly. 'Jonas and I are the ones who are leaving.'

His eyes widened at her determined tone, dark brows raised. 'We are?'

'Yes, we are,' she nodded. 'Contrary to what you said earlier, we—we have a wedding rehearsal to complete.' She was taking a gamble, the biggest gamble of her life, and the stakes were the highest she could possibly make—her future with Jonas.

He looked at her searchingly—hungrily?—a dark frown on his brows. Cassandra returned his piercing gaze steadily, although inside she was a quivering mass of uncertainty; what if she had gambled and lost? But at the same time she had nothing to lose; Jonas was going to leave here anyway if she didn't make some attempt to stop him, and take her future happiness with him, so there was nothing to lose and everything to gain if her gamble should by some miracle pay off. Something, besides her loss of temper earlier, had to have triggered off this change of heart in Jonas towards his family and their forced marriage.

'So we do,' he finally answered her huskily, and Cassandra began to breathe again—the first indication she had that she wasn't imagining this whole thing. Jonas turned to her mother. 'Don't worry about Hunter and Kyle, Marguerite,' he assured her dismissively. 'I will sort it out.'

'Cassandra?' Her mother looked at her uncertainly.

'As Jonas said, Mother, don't worry.' She squeezed her mother's hand reassuringly before kissing her on the cheek. 'I'll call you tomorrow morning,' she promised, glancing across at Jonas as she did so, her heart in her mouth at how wonderfully handsome he was, at how much she loved him...! 'Probably late morning,' she added decisively before releasing her mother's hand and turning to join Jonas. 'Shall we go?' she prompted huskily.

It wasn't until they got outside that Cassandra remembered they had arrived in separate cars. And she didn't want to be parted from Jonas just now—look what had happened the last time he had left her; she would hate him to revert back to that autocrat. 'We'll go in your car,' she told him firmly. 'I can always collect mine in the morning.'

'Cassandra——'

'Let's wait until we get back to the house, Jonas,' she pleaded. She needed time to gather her courage together for the next assault—because telling Jonas she loved him, or making him believe it, wasn't going to be easy! She had no idea what she would do, if at the end of all this he rejected that love. In fact, she couldn't even bear to think about that!

'Whatever you say.' He was surprisingly acquiescent—probably because he needed time to think things over too! She just hoped he didn't use the time to build back all those defences that made it so difficult for them to communicate over the things that were really important, such as how they really felt about each other...

Jean didn't seem in the least surprised to see the two of them arrive back together. After Jonas's earlier visit after Cassandra had already gone out, she probably thought it was perfectly natural for them to return together. After assuring them that Bethany hadn't stirred in their absence, she excused herself for the night.

Cassandra had been completely wrong in her belief that the drive home would give her time to gather her courage together for the conversation yet to come; she was as nervous as a young girl as she faced Jonas across the sitting-room. And Jonas looked as pale and tense as she felt! Where did she even begin to tell him how she felt about him?

'I love you, Cassandra Kyle Hunter.' He was the one to suddenly speak into the silence. 'And I've *never* said that to any other woman.'

All her nervousness, all her doubts, everything but the fact that this wonderful, magnificent man—she agreed whole-heartedly with Bethany!—loved her faded from her mind. 'Oh, Jonas!' she choked happily as she launched herself into his arms. 'I love you too. Oh, God, how I love you!' She rained kisses all over the hardness of his cheeks and jaw, laughing and crying at the same time—although both laughter and tears were erased as Jonas crushed her to him, his mouth fiercely claiming hers.

It was all there in that warmly exploring kiss—all his pent-up love for her, all the emotion he had shown her only with the touch of his lips and hands the night they made love. Because he *had* made love to her, no doubt about it; he had loved, adored and worshipped her body that night. As he loved, adored and worshipped her lips now.

'God!' He finally broke the kiss to rest his forehead against hers, his breathing ragged. 'I can't believe how much I love you, Cassandra,' he groaned. 'I took one look at you when I came back to England nine months ago and knew I wanted you for my own. And I despised myself for it. That was why I was such a bastard to you that first day we met,' he said grimly. 'Why I nurtured the hate I saw in your face that day for the things I was saying to you. I didn't *want* to love you. When I found out about the money missing from Hunter and Kyle— God, it seemed as if I would be able to have you for myself after all, without actually having to admit that I loved you!' He shook his head self-disgustedly. 'That's how determined I was not to make myself vulnerable to Charles's widow, of all people!'

Cassandra looked up at him with dazed eyes, her hands clinging to the hardness of his shoulders to stop herself from collapsing completely after the onslaught of his kiss. 'All this time...?' she said disbelievingly—not because she did disbelieve, but because it was so incredible!

'God, yes!' He gave a self-derisive grimace. 'And all I kept asking myself was what would I have done if I had come back for your wedding to Charles five years ago and felt the same way!' His eyes were dark with the pain of those agonising thoughts.

'I loved Charles, I'm not about to deny that I did,' she told him huskily. 'But—well, I had to be the strong one, and—it wasn't always easy.' She grimaced.

'I knew you loved him,' Jonas groaned. 'I think I've always known that. It was just easier for me to believe he had been fooled when he married you; that way I could even try to convince myself that you weren't worth loving either.' He shook his head sadly. 'It's much easier to hate than it is to love, Cassandra,' he admitted gruffly. 'Tonight, when I realised just how desperate you seemed to be to get out of marrying me, that you would even try to implicate Charles to do so——'

'But I really believed what I told you was true,' she protested, eyes dark with the memory of how she had

felt as if she was betraying Charles when she finally told
Jonas the truth.

Jonas nodded abruptly. 'Once I got away from here,
from you—for some reason you seem to cloud my
judgement,' he admitted ruefully, 'I sat and thought
about what you had said, and realised you really had
believed it was Charles you were protecting. I could see
by the genuine shock on your face, when I insisted it
wasn't, that that was true, and if you had believed that,
then there was only one person who could have told you
it: Charles himself. With that realisation I finally had
to admit that, selfish as I believe Charles was, he must
have loved you too, and by accepting that I also knew
that the grudge I've had against Charles and my father
for all these years was actually destroying any hope I
might have now of winning you for myself. But to do
that I had to first let you go——'

'I don't want you to let me go!' she told him fiercely,
her hands tightening on his shoulders.

'And I didn't really want to let you go either, but I
didn't feel at the time I had any choice!'

'And now?' She looked up at him anxiously.

His arms tightened about her. '*Now* I would like you
to be my wife willingly, lovingly. I want to have other
children with you, share with you, always, grow old with
you——'

'You'll never be old, Jonas.' She ran loving fingertips
down the hardness of his cheek. 'Never to me. And
you've already won me, my darling.' She smiled at him
emotionally. 'I think *I* took one look at *you* nine months
ago—and started running for my life!' she admitted
gruffly. 'Thank God you *didn't* come back five years

ago, Jonas, and put us all to that test; I'm not sure how it would have turned out!' She shook her head at the emotional dilemma that would have caused.

He looked down at her intently. 'Will you marry me, Cassandra? For all the right reasons this time!'

She smiled up at him through her tears. 'Only if sharing my bed is part of the deal!'

'No more deals, Cassandra,' he promised her huskily. 'And nothing will keep me out of your bed now that I know you love me! Although how you could possibly love the cruel bastard I've been to you——'

'You aren't cruel, Jonas.' She put silencing fingertips over his lips. 'You've just been hurt. And hurt people hit out. Especially at the people they care about.' Maybe she had always known that, which was why she had been able to hope that Jonas would ultimately come to care for her in return one day. She could still hardly believe he already loved her! 'I don't want you ever to be hurt again, Jonas,' she told him fiercely.

'I hurt right now, Cassandra.' His voice had lowered gruffly, and he moulded the length of her body to his, showing her all too clearly in what way he hurt!

'Then I'll have to take the pain away,' she murmured as she kissed the length of his jaw. 'Do you think we might make it as far as the bedroom this time?' she teased.

'Oh, I think we might.' He swung her up into his arms, his expression lovingly gentle as he looked down into her ecstatically happy face. 'I do love you, Cassandra, and I promise I'll spend the rest of my life showing you how much.'

Her arms encircled his neck. 'Start now. Please!'

He laughed softly, and it was the laughter of the triumphant hunter—the most beautiful sound Cassandra had ever heard...

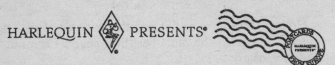

HARLEQUIN ◆ PRESENTS®

Harlequin Presents hopes you have enjoyed your year in Europe. If you missed any of the exciting countries on the tour, here is your opportunity to complete your collection:

Greece	#1619	*The Alpha Man* by Kay Thorpe	$2.99	☐
Italy	#1628	*Mask of Deception* by Sara Wood	$2.99	☐
Germany	#1636	*Designed To Annoy* by Elizabeth Oldfield	$2.99	☐
Spain	#1644	*Dark Sunlight* by Patricia Wilson	$2.99	☐
Belgium	#1650	*The Bruges Engagement* by Madeleine Ker	$2.99	☐
Italy	#1660	*Roman Spring* by Sandra Marton	$2.99 U.S. ☐ $3.50 CAN.☐
England	#1668	*Yesterday's Affair* by Sally Wentworth	$2.99 U.S. ☐ $3.50 CAN.☐
Portugal	#1676	*Sudden Fire* by Elizabeth Oldfield	$2.99 U.S. ☐ $3.50 CAN.☐
Cyprus	#1684	*The Touch of Aphrodite* by Joanna Mansell	$2.99 U.S. ☐ $3.50 CAN.☐
Denmark	#1691	*Viking Magic* by Angela Wells	$2.99 U.S. ☐ $3.50 CAN.☐
Switzerland	#1700	*No Promise of Love* by Lilian Peake	$2.99 U.S. ☐ $3.50 CAN.☐
France	#1708	*Tower of Shadows* by Sara Craven	$2.99 U.S. ☐ $3.50 CAN.☐

HARLEQUIN PRESENTS
NOT THE SAME OLD STORY!

TOTAL AMOUNT	$
POSTAGE & HANDLING	$
($1.00 for one book, 50¢ for each additional)	
APPLICABLE TAXES*	$ _____
TOTAL PAYABLE	$ _____
(check or money order—please do not send cash)	

To order, complete this form and send it, along with a check or money order for the total above, payable to Harlequin Books, to: **In the U.S.:** 3010 Walden Avenue, P.O. Box 9047, Buffalo, NY 14269-9047; **In Canada:** P.O. Box 613, Fort Erie, Ontario, L2A 5X3.

Name:_____

Address:_____ City:_____

State/Prov.:_____ Zip/Postal Code:_____

*New York residents remit applicable sales taxes.
Canadian residents remit applicable GST and provincial taxes.

HPPFE-F

This holiday, join four hunky heroes under the mistletoe for

Christmas Kisses

Cuddle under a fluffy quilt, with a cup of hot chocolate and these romances sure to warm you up:

#561 HE'S A REBEL (also a Studs title)
Linda Randall Wisdom

#562 THE BABY AND THE BODYGUARD
Jule McBride

#563 THE GIFT-WRAPPED GROOM
M.J. Rodgers

#564 A TIMELESS CHRISTMAS
Pat Chandler

Celebrate the season with all four holiday books sealed with a Christmas kiss—coming to you in December, only from Harlequin American Romance!